Inside the Lines

by
Ally Bishop

THANK YOU FOR EVERYTHING!

©2015 Ally Bishop

This work is licensed under a Creative Commons Attribution Noncommercial-No Derivative Works 3.0 Unported License.

Attribution--You must attribute the work in the manner specified by the author or licensor (but not in any way that suggests that they endorse you or your use of the work).

Noncommercial--You may not use this work for commercial purposes.

No Derivative Works--You may not alter, transform, or build upon this work with written consent from the author and/or publisher.

Inquiries about additional permissions should be directed to scarlet@scarletrivergroup.com

Cover Design by Ally Bishop

Edited by Patricia D. Eddy

Proofread by Audrey Maddox

This is a work of fiction. Names, characters, places, brands, media, and incidents are either the product of the author's imagination or are used fictitiously. Any resemblance to similarly named places or to persons living or deceased is unintentional.

Want some FREE sexy romances?

Sign up for my monthly newsletter and get the latest, plus early access to new books and special, members-only FREE romances!

To get started, click here:

www.allybishop.com

To Sir Prystauk, my knight in a shining white muscle car.
More than I can promise, my love.

Chapter 1

No Naughty Deed Goes Unpunished

This isn't my usual client.

Normally, they come to me. It's discreet and makes everyone's life easier. But for certain people, you make exceptions.

In the back of a sleek Lincoln Town Car, I relax into the leather as we enter the tunnel, heading for the famous Ritz Carlton. The car and driver are a courtesy of the client, and while it's not the first time I've had such treatment, I always enjoy it.

Deprived of scenery, I mentally review my gear, ensuring nothing is left to chance. Leather crop, purchased several years ago from a tack shop. Restraints in the form of scarlet cotton rope—silk ties are for movies and books. Entirely too slippery and time consuming. The usual detritus: blindfolds, clamps, rubber whips that range from noisy to pain-inducing. Sultry music, though I also brought a selection of classical entries on my iPad.

A quick check in my compact mirror assures me that the deep red lipstick I've fallen in love with provides the right contrast to my long, jet curls. My suit—pinstripe, skirted—fits my curves like a glove. Beneath, a dark leather and crimson corset meets a matching g-string, finished off with garters and stockings. Red stilettos complete the ensemble. The things I do for clients...

As we surface, I take a calming breath. There's always a bit of nerves right before an introductory scene. This client is new, and while I have a website with a photo gallery and specialties listed, each person's sexual desires are like snowflakes: while similar in appearance to others, each has their own unique intricacies.

Topping—or playing the Dom—requires you to know your bottom, or submissive. You can't push too hard or too far, as you risk injuring not only your client, but also the relationship, that's tenuous at the beginning. At the same time, if you go too light, or God forbid, too slowly, you lose future profits and referrals.

A balancing act. That's the best way to describe it. Sometimes, I wish I could be a submissive. A friend who enjoys playing the slave once told me that she loves turning inward, focusing on her own interests and pleasures, while the Dom does all the work. God, I wish I could let someone else run the show. But that's not the way it works. Or rather, not the way I operate.

Traffic in New York City is always brutal this time of day, but the driver gets a few lucky breaks. As he navigates the crowded streets, I go over my notes, replay my client's application video on my phone, and try to gauge his personality and true desires.

Creating—or recreating—someone's fantasies requires imagination and research, but it also relies on innate skills. For this client, I have a pretty good idea of what he wants.

Who am I kidding? I know exactly what he wants. Because in reality, all of my clients want the same thing.

To let go. To be in the moment. To escape life.

Sounds amazing, doesn't it? I envy them in so many ways.

The driver drops me off at the entrance. The Ritz Carlton isn't your average hotel — I probably don't have to tell you that. The lobby defines elegance, with sleek lighting, antique furniture with a modern flair, and a quiet confidence that bespeaks the well-to-do that venture here.

I visit the concierge on duty and receive an envelope from him. The elevator doors snick shut behind me, and I slip behind the crowd, falling against the back wall and closing my eyes. For once, my outfit doesn't draw hushed comments, as besides the skirt that barely covers my ass, I'm pretty low-key in a city of models and movie stars. Okay, maybe the shoes stick out a bit, too.

The elevator is empty by the time I reach the top public floor. Penthouse access requires a special passkey, and I extract mine from the envelope and slide it into the card reader. Then I wait while the elevator's silken glide ferries me to the penthouse floor.

Stepping onto the lush carpet, I have two doors to choose from. I feel a bit like Alice in Wonderland until I remember the room number the client texted me earlier today. With the Pixies' "Where Is My Mind?" forming an earworm in my brain, I knock.

A delicious man opens the door. Thick, dark hair, lightly threaded with silver, strong jaw with an aquiline nose, sultry eyes that take in the length of me. He wears an exquisitely tailored suit that cuts across his impossibly broad shoulders in a mix of elegance and power. When he smiles, even my jaded heart quivers a bit.

"Mistress Hathaway. A pleasure."

I level a gaze at him, knowing that my raven curls and gray eyes captivate my clients. "The pleasure will be mine, Charles. Naughty boys have to be punished."

As a professional Dominatrix, I follow three rules:
1. Never let them disobey you.
2. Never let them touch you.
3. Never have sex with them.

At least, I used to follow them...

Chapter 2
Caffeinated Confessions

"Oh, God. Tell me the coffee is ready."

I grin at my roommate's dramatic entrance, then check the clock. It's 8 a.m. now, and I vaguely heard him crawl in around four this morning. Given his current marathon of one-night stands... "Rough night, eh, Romeo?"

Noah drops his hand from his eyes to scowl at me. "You know fucking well that I had a client party last night, wench."

"I never know with you. Party one night, orgy the next—"

He groans. "I'm a one woman kinda guy. You're the one with the resume in orgies."

"One woman per night, you mean." With a laugh, I get up and hold out my chair. "Take a load off, and I'll even get you a cuppa."

Sinking into the seat, he slumps. "I take it all back. You are a goddess."

I refill my own mug and then mix Noah's with lots of half-and-half and sugar. Wuss.

"How was your evening?" he asks as I hand him his favorite extra dark roast that's now nearly white with creamer.

"Better than yours, it appears."

"Really? What can top cleaning up not one, but two vomiting episodes courtesy of a host whose religious friends have no tolerance for alcohol?"

Noah and his sister are co-owners of Elementary, a mystery dinner party company. Their business has exploded over the last year after gaining some celebrity clients, and while they now have a team of coordinators and planners, they both personally handle the more prestigious bookings.

"Hm, let's see: torturing one of the handsomest men in all of Christendom?"

He sticks out his tongue. "Rub it in."

I grab the newspaper off the front walkway and return to the kitchen table. We split up the paper, Noah taking the comics and the sports sections, while I peruse the international and local news. We're both engrossed by the time the front door opens again.

"Tell me there's coffee," comes the voice of Noah's sister, Ella. When she finally appears in the kitchen, she's wearing jeans and a short-sleeve sweater with a suspicious stain on her shoulder. "You know I love my child. I adore her. But someone tell me that she will eventually sleep through the night?" Despite the faint purple smudges under her eyes, Ella is stunning with her long, dark hair wrapped into a sloppy french twist and pale skin. Even after having her daughter Mia, she manages to look dewy and gorgeous.

"I'm told they do, but I wouldn't know from personal experience." I leave my paper spread over the table and head for another cup of coffee.

I return to the table with her favorite mug.

"You are a goddess," she says as she takes her first sip.

"In case I ever forget that you and Noah are related..."

"What?" they both ask at the same time.

"Yeah, that."

Confused, they stare at me, but I shake my head. "I will get no peace now that y'all are together, so go forth: make crazy money and build your business to monstrous proportions, you nutty capitalists. I'll be in my room until...well, whenever."

I drop a kiss on Ella's head before I take shelter upstairs. I moved in with Noah about eight months ago, not long after Ella moved out to marry the love of her life. It wasn't just a financial decision—I've taken care of myself for years, and Noah had just started to make a good income with Elementary—though affording a place anywhere near New York City isn't easy. Noah and Ella lost their parents in a car crash when they were teens, and as a result, have lived together all of their lives.

They even went to college together—that's where I met them. So being alone didn't sit well with him. When I mentioned my lease was ending and I was considering moving to a bigger place, Noah offered me Ella's old room. Their apartment, tucked into the bottom two stories of a Brooklyn brownstone, is spacious—for NYC—and has plenty of room for two people. It helped that we were friends already. With the exception of the occasional annoyance over laundry duty or who last changed the toilet paper roll, it's worked out pretty well.

But...

For someone who's always lived on her own terms, even *I'm* getting tired of putting up with me all the time. I've tried relationships. I even had a (very) brief live-in thing with a really nice guy a little over a year ago. It never works out. Not for me. And I'm not even sure there's a solution to any of it. I've always been happy being alone. But the last year or so, I've felt this internal pressure to settle down, find that special someone. Lonely, even. And you'd think it would be easier for someone like me: I'm open to men or women, and I'm sexually interested in many different lifestyles and kinks. I thought perhaps living with someone, albeit a roommate, might alleviate some of the loneliness. But it hasn't. Noah's great, but he's like a brother to me. I want a lover and a soulmate.

God, I sound pathetic even to myself.

So rather than deal with the frustration, I pick up a magazine and lose myself in the latest celebrity gossip and movie reviews.

It's late afternoon when I poke my head in on Noah and Ella in the dining-room-turned-Elementary headquarters. "Did someone say lunch? I could have sworn I heard the shuffling of takeout menus."

Ella glances up from her MacBook. "Oh God, yes. Food. And I have to pump, anyway."

Ah, the joys of motherhood.

Noah remains tied to his laptop, so I sneak over to take a peek. "What is this? Online dating?"

He immediately slams the lid shut. "Privacy much?"

I prop my hand on my hip. "Damn. Who would have thought Don Juan of the One Night Stand would be looking for love. What gives, T-bone?"

The nickname both annoys and entertains him, and the two responses war for dominance across his features. "If you must know, I'm doing some research for a friend."

Ella, who's disappeared into the kitchen to use her breast pump, snorts loudly. "If that isn't the oldest excuse in the book, I don't know what is."

Noah runs a hand through his thick, dark hair. "God save me from meddling women."

"Aw, you wuv us," I say with saccharine in my voice. "You could let us have a quick look. We could probably tell you who is blowing smoke, and who's a good bet."

"I'm good, thanks. I can figure it out on my own."

"Famous last words," Ella adds from the other room.

He shakes his head, but refuses to say more.

"Well, since I stumbled onto your little secret, I'll tell you mine." Even giving the words life makes my stomach flutter.

"Hey! Wait for me, dammit," echoes from the kitchen.

"Let's order. Then you give us the details." Noah reaches for the preponderance of food options tucked behind his computer. We pore over the menus, debate sides and appetizers, negotiate spiciness and substitutions with all the seriousness of three people planning an itinerary for their once-in-a-lifetime trip to Europe. Once we get our dietary needs squared away and Ella finishes, we settle into the living room to await our food.

Ella collapses on the largest couch and drops her head in my lap. "The floor is yours, gorgeous."

I run my fingers over her scalp, smiling as her eyes close. "Well...I have an idea. At least, it's part of an idea."

Noah swings his legs over the end of the small couch and lets his slippers dangle off his feet. "And?" he prods when I don't continue.

I wear patent leather from head to foot and cane men twice my size. Yet sharing my guts with my best friends makes me nervous. But then, there's more than just this to tell them, isn't there? I've always shared my guts with them, but for once in our friendship, I'm keeping secrets. I immediately extinguish that mode of thinking. I love Ella and Noah dearly, but my morality and ethics about who I sleep with are my own to decide. At least, that's what I keep telling myself.

The doorbell buys me time, and Noah grabs the food. With lunch dispensed on the coffee table and utensils in hand, I start to feel a bit calmer.

"So what's the big news?" Ella arches an eyebrow.

"I don't really know how big it is," I say after I take my first bite of lo mein. I inhale a deep breath, then plunge ahead. "So I have an idea of creating an online dating service for kinksters called Kinked. Like a matchmaking setup to help people find others with their fetishes or interests." I blow out a breath. Giving my entrepreneurial dream a voice both excites and terrifies me.

"Ooo," Ella coos.

"Sounds fantastic," Noah agrees. "What's stopping you?"

"Nothing yet, as I'm still just thinking about it. Actually doing it… well, it's going to be expensive, and I need to finish my business plan, find investors…. It's not like what you guys did with Elementary." I tuck a lock of hair behind my ear. "I don't have the Noah-and-Ella-Storm-voodoo-magic on my side, so I can't do it grass-roots-style and create it all on my own. I'd have to have an online component and significant advertising. It has to look classy from the start, no exceptions."

"You'll always have the 'Storm-magic-voodoo-whatever-you-called-it' on your side," Ella says with a pointed look as she curls a leg under her. "What's the competition? Does anything like that already exist?"

I make a face. "God, yes, and they're awful and cheesy. That's why Kinked has to be different. Better. Elegant."

They both turn thoughtful, with only the sound of our chewing punctuating the silence. We're nearly done with the fried rice when Ella drops her head as though she's come to a decision. "Noah can review your business plan. He's a whiz at those, and I can help you with marketing. I'd also like to invest in your idea. I'm sure Ian will agree."

How is it I've spent months, maybe even a year, flipping this idea over in my head, yet within minutes, Ella has it all planned out? This is why I doubt my ability to do this—for once, I don't know all the rules, and given that I've made a career out of sexual fantasies, maybe I have no business even contemplating it?

Ella's expression suggests she knows she's hit a nerve. "Lux, I'm not trying to take over. I'm just excited for you."

"I know. And I love you for it." I squeeze her arm. "Thanks for your vote of confidence. I need to make sure I'm 100% committed to it, as well. This would certainly put a kink in my current schedule, pun intended."

Ella smiles. "Of course. I just think it's a great idea and can't wait for you to get started."

Noah nods in agreement. "Let us know how we can help."

I take a final bite of lo mein, then gather up my trash. "I should let you two get back to work." I check the clock on the cable box. "Besides, I gotta get ready for tonight in a bit."

Ella grabs my hand as I get up. "It's a great idea, Lux. When you're ready, we're here to help."

I squeeze her fingers, then step back. "I know. And I appreciate it. I just gotta wrap my head around it, you know? I'm not the entrepreneur that you two are. The idea of interacting with people as a business entity and having employees..." I mock-shiver.

Noah chuckles, his dark eyes teasing. "Oh, please. It will be just like having a whole team of slaves to do your bidding. What Dominatrix wouldn't love that?"

I smile. "You make a very good point, my minion. A very good point."

Later, as I pack my work bag, worries about Kinked return. While Ella and Noah's response to my idea is reassuring, it digs up a whole other set of concerns. What the hell am I thinking? I've been a professional Dominatrix for...five years? Six? I've worked in corporate America, and I didn't belong there. This was the first thing I found that resonated with my soul. While starting Kinked doesn't mean I have to give everything up, I've watched Noah and Ella build Elementary, and they worked on it day and night. Ella wasn't even sure she could have a relationship and a family while still being an active CEO in her own company. She's made it work...but she has Noah and Ian to pick up the slack. I've got me. And if the ball drops, there's no one else to catch it.

Not to mention, with my latest faux pas concerning my work rules, I'm not bringing my A-game to the table. I would never admit this to anyone, but I'm a little worried about *me*. I've never played this far outside the lines before—and that's saying something for someone who lives outside them—and I'm not sure that I can tread water much longer.

This mindset does nothing for the scene I'm setting tonight. As I walk towards the subway, I dig out my earbuds and listen to some haunting, wordless music. Deep, slow breaths help center me and focus my thoughts on the powerful night ahead. The rest of it—Kinked, my relationship worries, my doubts about my own abilities—doesn't matter. What I am and have always been good at is controlling a situation and giving people their fantasies. I embrace that as I head off into the night.

Chapter 3

Substitutions

You are never going to believe me when I say that I work out of a dungeon space I keep on reserve, but I swear that's usually the case. But in this specific situation, I am, once again, going to the client. Tonight is a very special evening.

I arrive at the Parisienne Hotel, one of the newest hotels in Soho. This evening's client wanted something romantic and chic, and the Parisienne Hotel fits the bill, while not breaking the bank.

Everything about the hotel is European, from the creamy decor to the extravagant chandeliers that line the ceiling. I'm early, as intended, so I check-in and head for the far alcove. My stomach drops in time to the quick lift of the elevator, and I swallow hard. While I usually have a bit of nerves before a scene, this one comes with complications.

I wasn't kidding about my three rules. They've served me well. Somewhere along the way, though, I started breaking the last one. Fuck it; I'll be honest. It happened after my relationship with Evan ended. He was—and is—a sweetheart. Good looking, submissive, kind, loving, talented…the list goes on. He's what every healthy, normal woman wants in a really nice guy. It wasn't enough for me. I wanted it to be—so badly, I wanted it to be enough. But I couldn't do it. He deserved someone who loved all of him, completely. And I couldn't do that. So I let go of him. Pushed him away, really, because he'd wanted to continue dating.

Something about that experience angered me. It created a resentment that's hard to describe. So when a long-time client of mine booked me to join him in a scene with another couple, I did something I never do: I got involved sexually. It was delicious, and I had an amazing time. Limiting your sex life to only what you can create with one lover when you consistently create sexual energy for others is draining. And that experience reminded me that I had this raw need inside, and that it could be sated.

The downside: I had sex with several people. And got paid for it. I didn't like the way that part made me feel. That hasn't stopped me from doing it again and again. With only a select few clients, of course. I'm not a prostitute, for fuck's sake.

But then...what am I?

The candescence of pink light softens the room. The hazy glow turns the blood red decor into a deep maroon. This hotel made a splash because of its "red suites;" they're swanky and beautifully styled. And for this evening's pleasure, they seemed like the perfect fit. I've remade the suite's bedroom with the softer bulbs, draping scarves, red boas, and a few well-placed, cotton restraints.

Someone knocks, and I hope it's Stephen. But when I open the door, it's Ari.

"Oh, God, am I too early?" Her blue eyes go round as she takes in my cut up t-shirt that falls artfully, exposing my shoulder, and stops just shy of my wine-colored skinny jeans.

"Well, it's not quite—" I check my phone for the time but also see a missed text, which makes me frown. "What the..." Apparently, I nudged the ringer off, and with setting up and moving around, I missed the vibration of a new text. One that says Stephen can't make it. "Un-fucking-believable. You asshole."

Ari stares at me, wide-eyed. Her white-blond hair shimmers in a short, wispy cut that frames her heart-shaped face. A professional dancer, Ari has the slight build of a ballerina, but with more softness and curve.

I shake my head. "Not you, love. Come in. You're about a half hour early, so I haven't changed yet. Come in," I say again when she pauses at the door. One of the ongoing problems with Ari is her hesitance. It's taken me nearly six months to get her to this point. I'm going to kill Stephen for ruining it.

I check the text so I can read the whole thing.

Sry, dove, I'm sick. And u don't want my snot ruining a sexy scene. Found a replacement, tho. Fin. Trust me, u will luv him. xoxo.

I receive a second text as I'm standing there.

Hi. It's Fin. Stephen sent me. I'm here at the hotel. What room?

Un-fucking-believable. I text him the floor and say I'll meet him. Then I return Stephen's message: *you better die of this illness. Or I promise, you'll wish you did.*

"Ari, I'll be right back. Make yourself comfortable. Remember what we talked about. Deep breaths, center yourself—"

"Envision, and repeat mantra." Ari's light voice finishes for me. "I know." She smiles, but the corners of her mouth flicker with nerves.

Inwardly, I sigh. Then I shower her with smiling confidence and step into the hallway, closing the door snugly.

When the elevator opens, another couple gets off, wheeling luggage behind them. The doors start to shut, but then a strong hand holds them open. The man that steps off is very tall, well over six feet, and when his aquamarine eyes meet mine, he grins.

"Lux, I take it?" His deep voice holds a heavy Scottish burr. He wears jeans and a nondescript black t-shirt under a black leather jacket, and if I weren't so mad, I'd be swooning. Dear God. His shoulders and chest are broad, but not thick. He's built more like a soccer player, with wavy auburn hair with hints of chestnut. He has a crooked smile, and when I stand there staring for a moment, I get a glimpse of perfectly straight teeth and a dimple.

Holy Christ. Stephen sent me an underwear model.

"I know you. You're the guy from that ad. Th-the new Monsieur line. You're on the goddamn billboard in Times Square in bikini briefs." Monsieur is a male clothing boutique on Fashion Avenue; they've been making quite a stir with their advertising of everyday men—e.g. not celebrities or models, though you'd be hard-pressed to find one that isn't ripped— wearing their new underwear line.

His cheeks blush, which on him, is highly attractive, and I get more of that uneven grin. "Aye, well, that might've been me." He scratches the back of his neck. "Stephen said ye needed a bit of help tonight."

And with that, I remember how pissed I am. "Stephen is a goddamn asshole. Do you even know what you're doing here tonight? Did he give you the details?" If there is one thing I'm sensing, it's a distinct lack of kink. Fin looks like he should have a blonde wife, 2.5 kids, and a house with a white picket fence.

"Well, he wasna very specific with details, but he did mention that ye needed a cock." His eyes crinkle even more at his bald language, his face turning brighter pink. "Seein' as which I have one of those, I should be able to help ye." His brogue thickens with his embarrassment.

"Christ. I'm glad Stephen narrowed the whole evening down to a male organ." I glare at Fin. "Men." I turn and storm away, leaving Fin to follow. I feel like I have an enormous shadow behind me, and I realize I have to have this conversation away from the room's door, or Ari will hear it. So I turn on my heel and confront him mid-hallway.

I crane my neck to make eye contact. "Never mind. Just go home. I'm canceling this nightmare before it gets out of hand."

He lays a hand on my shoulder as I turn away, his heat searing my bare skin. "Wait, now. Look." He drops his hand and stops a beat until I meet his gaze. "I ken I'm not the charmer Stephen is, but I ken a fair bit about what he does. I think I can handle it. And he mentioned that ye were a Dominatrix, and that ye'd be runnin' things, so ye can just tell me what to do." He bites the inside of his lip. "I'll do it."

The cheer in his eyes pisses me off. "This is a joke to you. You can barely keep from laughing." I shake my head at him, my temper undoubtedly turning my own skin pink. "This is not funny. The woman on the other side of that door," I point down the hallway, "is terrified of letting herself go. She has a hard time enjoying sex because of assholes who ridiculed and abused her rather than making her feel beautiful and aroused. I will be damned if I will let you anywhere near her. Not when you think this is some kind of goddamn joke. You are—"

"Lux, I'm sorry. I wasna laughing at ye or anything about this." He steps closer, and I get a whiff of some kind of creamy, spicy cologne mixed with...him, probably. And it's delicious. "But ye have a feather here," his hand reaches towards my hair and plucks something from it. "And it wiggles, the angrier ye get."

I glare at the offending feather and snatch it from him. It's from one of the props I brought with me, and the delicate fringe crushes easily in my palm. I close my eyes and take a deep breath. If I cancel this, Ari will be heartbroken. I've fielded half a dozen texts from her already this week, thanking me for doing this and asking nervous questions. After six months of meeting with her, we're finally at the point of fulfilling her deepest fantasy. And there are worse-looking men to have in your fantasy than this one.

"You cannot, I repeat, *cannot* fuck this up. You listen to me, you do exactly what I say, and you never step a toe out of line. Am I clear?" Even to my ears, I sound like a total ass, but surprisingly, Fin only nods.

"Aye."

"You will call me Mistress Hathaway, as none of my clients know my real name."

"Of course."

"You'll strip down to your underwear when we get inside, and you will not approach the bedroom or Ari until I say so. Got it?"

He nods, his face solemn, though I can still see the laughter in his eyes. "After ye, Mistress," he says with a small bow.

Chapter 4

Three's a Crowd

After I've briefed Fin on his role in tonight's scene—with hopefully less ire than I displayed in the hallway—I retire to the bathroom to change into my own garb. I selected a deep scarlet corset with black thigh-high nylons and black stilettos. I tie my hair in a side ponytail, the long, inky curls relaxing over my breast. Satisfied, I join Ari in the bedroom.

I introduce her to Fin, who was waiting in the separate living area. He is just as devastating out of his clothes as he was in them. Muscles borne of hard work bulge beneath a light tan, and if I weren't on the clock, I would totally drool. This is a job. And I am, if nothing else, a professional. Even if I do notice that he has a phenomenal ass.

"Ari, you've asked for this experience today because you wish to embrace your submissive side. This means that no matter what happens here, you are safe. You will be obedient, do what you are told, and you will be pleasured. If at any time, you want us to stop, you may use your safe word. Do you remember it?" It seems like a silly thing to ask, but nerves can ruin memories.

Ari takes a deep breath before answering. "Pepper, Mistress."

I smile my approval, but glance at Fin to make sure he's paying attention. His focus is on the discussion, and he nods slightly to me.

"Any questions, Fin?" Ari doesn't know that he's a substitute. As far as she knows, he's exactly whom I planned to be here.

"No, Mistress."

I quell the doubts in my gut. "Then we begin."

Ari chose a stunning bra and panty set, a peachy-pink netting accented with luminous beads. In my heels, I tower over her small stature, so it's easy for me to draw her to me. She's shaking, and I hold her close, letting her relax. After a few minutes, her breathing slows, and though her fingers are still cool with nerves, she turns her head up eagerly as I tip her mouth to mine.

I've made love to Ari before. She was the first client with whom I broke my rules. Then and now, she tastes faintly of raspberries, and as I deepen our kiss, she mews in the back of her throat. I hold her hands behind her back, using my other hand to outline her jaw and neck. When I pull back to gauge her reaction, her eyes open slightly, but she's completely relaxed. I lower my mouth to hers again, exploring her with my tongue.

Fin steps beside us, his body emanating heat as he trails his hands along Ari's shoulders and back. Pressing kisses against her neck, his hands brush mine, and I feel a bit of a thrill deep in my stomach. Whatever else Fin may be, he knows how to tease and caress a woman. Ari moans softly as I kiss her cheek and jaw.

With gentle pressure, I nudge her towards the bed, Fin stepping back to make room. I stand her between us, then return to her mouth as he unhooks her bra. I cover her small breasts with my hands, their centers rising against my palms.

"What do you want, Ari?" I whisper in her ear.

She whimpers as my fingers lightly pinch her nipples. "To be tied down, Mistress."

I know how hard it was for her to say that, and she vibrates a bit as I edge her towards the bed. But she lies down on it obediently, centering herself on the king mattress. I've already prepared the soft restraints on either side of the bed. I glance at Fin, his signal to confine her one wrist while I tie the other.

Properly subdued, I step back and admire the symmetry of Ari's bound wrists and the glow of her skin under the soft lights. She's truly beautiful, but when I glance over at Fin, he's peering at me with an odd intensity. I resist a shiver, though my core quivers despite my determination to remain unaffected.

I slide up beside Ari, teasing her with kisses as I straddle her. "Are you ready to come for me, Ari?"

Bending to her nipple, I draw it between my lips, sucking it hard as she arches against my mouth. "Yes, Mistress. Please," she groans between breaths.

With a quick exchange of looks, Fin joins us on the bed, on Ari's other side. He kisses her, his large hands holding her face. I continue to torture her breasts until he moves down beside me, Ari's body writhing as we each tease a nipple.

My fingers drift over her stomach, outlining the edge of her panties. I leave Fin to her breasts and divert my attention lower. Sliding her panties off, I nudge her thighs apart, letting my fingers graze the edge of her outer lips. Ari's sharp intake of breath is quickly followed by, "Please."

"Please what, Ari?"

Moments pass while I circle her sensitive skin with my finger, refusing to give her more until she answers me. Fin surprises me by moving to her mouth, kissing her deeply before encouraging her. "Ye must answer yer Mistress, love."

She finally whispers, "Please fuck me, Mistress."

With her obedience comes a reward, so I slide my fingers into her wet pussy, her juices coating them as they move against her. I use my thumb to tease her clit, and her whole body thrums with arousal, her hips bucking against my hand as her arms strain against the cotton ropes. I lower myself between her legs, lightly nipping the tender skin of her inner thigh. When my mouth covers her, she cries out, and I hold her hips in place so I can lap her clit with gentle strokes. A glimpse of movement distracts me as Fin moves down Ari's body to worship her breasts again.

My fingers fill her once more as she twists and moans. When she finally reaches her release, Ari is nearly hoarse with her cries. I press my tongue hard against her, my fingers penetrating even deeper, as she shudders and gives in to her rapture. I stroke her thigh, the silky skin covered in a sheen of sweat. When she's recovered her breath, I stand, giving Fin room. He strips out of his briefs, powerful muscles shifting as he stands before me.

The back of my throat goes a bit dry at the sight of him—gorgeous men are always appealing. But he's built, with visible abs and a narrow waist. If I wasn't already wet, I would be from the sight of him. His gaze meets mine, his mouth pulled into a knowing grin. Remembering myself, I straighten, then bend to Ari while Fin readies a condom.

"You did well." I press a kiss to her lips, and she surges into me, mouth hot and hungry. Her excitement assures me that this is going well, so I pull back. "You are ready for what comes next." I say it, rather than ask, though I'm watching her expression to make sure.

She smiles, meeting my eyes. "Yes, Mistress, I am."

Fin situates himself between her pale thighs, adjusting her so that her legs dangle over his arms. There is no more alluring sight than watching this union, and when his hard cock sinks into Ari, my own stomach curls with anticipation.

He sets a gentle pace, and Ari groans with her enjoyment. I explore her mouth, letting her tongue reach for mine. With fingers tugging her nipples, I feel her sharp intake of breath.

"Oh God," Ari breathes. "I'm going to come again."

I grin. "Good girl. Come for me, Ariana. I want to hear you." She suckles a finger I place in her mouth, her moans increasing in volume.

Fin shifts her legs so her thighs are pressed against his chest, giving him deeper purchase as he fucks her harder. Ari's panted groans grow more frenzied until she shouts her climax. Fin continues, though, his measured strokes picking up speed.

"God, no, I can't," Ari whispers, but her body has other plans. I slip my hand between them, enjoying the feel of Fin's cock against my fingers as he enters Ari. Then I rub her engorged clit, sending Ari into yet another orgasm. Fin joins her, his own groan of satisfaction ringing in my ears, and when I look at him as they both come down from their pleasure, I realize that he's been looking at me the whole time.

Well-fucked and dressed, Ari joins me in the living area. "I don't know how to thank you, Mistress Hathaway. That was…incredible." She smiles, but tears hint at the corners of her eyes.

Her happiness means more than I can say, and I have to fight the emotion. Instead, I hug her, and she squeezes me tight. "I'm so proud of you," I whisper.

She offers Fin a coy smile and an outstretched hand. "And thank you for making it special."

He takes her hand, and in a surprisingly gallant gesture, presses a soft kiss to her knuckles. "It was my privilege, m'lady."

Ari's pale cheeks are bright pink as she leaves. I feel triumphant. After nearly six months of counsel and conversation, Ari finally embraced her fantasy. I turn to Fin with a nod. "Thanks for being a gentleman tonight. You made it very special for her."

"Thank ye for letting me take part." His accent tumbles over the words, giving them warmth that matches his shy grin.

I nod. "You can go."

Apparently unaccustomed to being dismissed, he hesitates. "Can I help ye gather yer things?"

"Nope. I'm good. It won't take long. Tell Stephen he's lucky he found a good replacement." I wink to soften the words, and then turn my back to evaluate the room.

I hear the door close behind him, and I can finally breathe a sigh of relief. Deep down, the niggling of my conscience remains—for all the win that tonight represents for Ari, that I am having sex with my clients remains a problem I need to deal with.

Chapter 5
Girl Talk

"Wait, so you mean a hot, polite man just showed up—Scottish, no less—and you didn't get his name and number? Who are you, and where have you taken my best friend?" Ella insists as we soak our feet in scalding, bubbling water.

I sit back in the pedicure chair, closing my eyes and ignoring Ella's disbelief. We'd agreed to meet for pedicures, as between the craziness of her work schedule with Elementary and Mia, we rarely got in any girl time. Now I regret telling her about last night. Well, I only told her about the Fin part of last night.

"You liked him."

I snort. "He was a rented dick, Ells. He did the job."

"You've mentioned him several times, including how good-looking he is." She gave me a meaningful look. "I recognize the signs of a Lux Trace crush."

"Please. Like you would even know." It sounds harsh even to my ears, but I'm wildly uncomfortable with her assumption. Did I say a lot about him? I might have mentioned his physique and accent a few times. A crush? Hardly.

Hmph.

"I daresay I would," she responds dryly. "In the eight years I've known you, there was Rob, Taylor, Guy, Rob number two, Jon, Jonathan, Jason, Justin, Eric, Evan—" She counts them off on her fingers.

I open my eyes and hold up a hand. "Point made." Jesus, have I really dated that many men since college? And those are just the Facebook status-update ones. Because I'm pretty sure there are a few more on top of the ones she mentioned, and that doesn't include recreational sexy times. Damn. "And all that proves is that I need to swear off dating. I can't make a single relationship work." Evan was the closest I'd come to being happy, and even that hadn't been enough.

She widens her eyes in surprise. "Lux…you just haven't met the right person."

I shrug, then slosh my feet around the hot water. This deluxe pedicure chair offers a light show of colors in the water, so I focus on that rather than respond to Ella.

After a few moments, she lets it go. "So, any more thoughts about Kinked?"

The word itself causes a flutter in my gut. "I'm almost done with the business plan. Noah said he'd review it tomorrow. It's still pretty intense, you know?"

"I think it's a great idea. Plus, it would put you more in charge of your career."

"What's that supposed to mean? I'm already in charge of my career."

Her blue eyes soften. "That was a bad choice of words, Lux. I'm sorry."

The sincerity in her voice shames me. Am I that hung up and miserable lately that I'm popping off at my best friend when she's just trying to be helpful? "I'm the one who should be sorry. And I am. I'm in a bad head space right now. It makes me cranky."

She takes my hand and squeezes my fingers. "Anything I can do?"

I return the gesture, then pull my hand from her grasp. "Nope. Just gotta get through it. Tell me about the small one."

Her face lights up. "Which part? About how adorable and delicious she is? Or how exhausted she makes me?" She feigns sleep. "I feel like I could sleep for a month. Oh, but let me show you…" She digs out her phone and pulls up her photo album. "Look at Mia's face this morning. Oh my gosh, her dimples are killer. Just like her daddy's."

She shows me at least fifteen photos of the baby. She's adorable, but that's hardly surprising given her parents. I make the appropriate ohs and ahs over her pictures while I fight the envy that comes from seeing my friend's joy; in many ways, it's another reminder of how far away I am from having anything like that.

"You okay?"

I must've been silent for too long. "Of course. I'm just blown away by your beauteous child." I offer a small smile in the hopes that she'll forgive me.

One amazing thing about Ella—she always does. As the pedicurist returns to pretty-up our feet, she leans over and kisses me on the cheek. "I'm here for you, you know."

I nod, once again overcome with emotions I don't have anywhere to go with.

Charles requested a standing appointment with me. While I'm never one to turn down a regular, I'm surprised he made a decision that quickly. Most of my regular clients took a few weeks to warm up to having a regular meeting with a Mistress. Of course, he seems to be a man who understands his preferences and needs, based on our first meeting.

After our second session, I slip back into my trench coat and situate myself on the sofa in the suite's living room. That is another surprise with Charles—he has no desire to meet at my dungeon. Instead, he pays for an extravagant room at one of the most expensive hotels in the city. Hey, I'm not going to argue with him. Less clean up and room rental for me.

He dries his hands on a towel as he rejoins me in the living area. "Thank you, Mistress Hathaway. Once again, you astound me with your skill."

I bow my head slightly. "Thank you, Charles. You were very well-behaved today. More so than the first session."

His handsome face turns slightly embarrassed. "Yes, I admit, your punishment takes a bit to get used to. You have a firm hand with the whip." When I don't smile, he rushes to finish, "Which I greatly appreciate."

I bestow a small grin, then stand. "It's been my pleasure, Charles."

"Would you mind having a cup of coffee with me? And I'm not propositioning you, Mistress Hathaway. I was wondering if you'd mind, when we meet, enjoying a few moments of conversation afterwards? You may charge me whatever you wish for your time."

His request surprises me, but I don't sense any flirtation from him. He seems to want nothing more than a cup of coffee. It's an odd question, and I'd normally turn such a request down. But I hear myself say, "For a few minutes."

Room service comes within moments. Coffee dispensed, I sit back on the sofa and eye him where he reclines in a chair. "So what did you wish to talk about?"

For the first time, he's a bit self-conscious, and he slides a hand through his wavy hair. "I was hoping you'd tell me more about your work. I was… in a relationship with a Dominatrix years ago, but she… I'm not sure of a polite way to say it, so I'll just be blunt. She wasn't a healthy person. She took it too far, often, to the point that she had a breakdown. I've always wondered how you balance what you do against your relationships? How do you embrace who you are in a world that is less than welcoming?"

His question hits me in an uncomfortable place. I wouldn't call myself the poster child for balancing your proclivities. He's right: some people lose themselves in the BDSM world in an effort to avoid dealing with life. "I'm not sure I have the answer you are looking for, Charles. I've been involved in the BDSM world since I was a teenager. But I didn't find myself there to avoid anything, either. I was drawn to it because it spoke to who I knew I was. Does that make sense?"

With a nod, he takes a sip of his coffee. "Perfectly. I always questioned whether she really *was* a Dom, or if she chose that road to avoid being hurt."

"That very well may be. She wouldn't be the first person I've heard of who did so." Sadness haunts his eyes. "You loved her."

After a pause, he nods slowly. "I did. Very much."

I sigh. "I'm so sorry. This must have been hard for you—to seek me out."

"It was… the first time I sought out someone to meet my needs in several years, yes."

"I'm glad you did."

"May I ask you one more question?"

The coffee still steams in the cup, so I nod. "Of course."

"I don't mean to be impertinent, and you may tell me it is none of my business. Have you found a way to have this," he motions to the bedroom, "and a healthy relationship at the same time? I've met quite a few people who engage in BDSM, but they've either not lasted as a couple, or they've found partners that allow them to play with others, rather than bring it home."

"That's an excellent question. I have met people who are able to 'balance' it, and quite successfully. So I wouldn't give up hope. But I've yet to find that harmony for myself."

"Ah. Yes. Well, that does give me some measure of hope. Thank you, Mistress."

We finish our coffee discussing banal bits of news and culture. When I take my leave, he walks me to the door, then holds his hands out to me. I place my fingers against his large, warm palms.

"Thank you, Mistress Hathaway. I will endeavor to be less naughty for you."

"Very good, Charles. Until the next time."

Many of my clients have little routines they like after a session, so Charles is not unusual in that. But there's an elegance to him that makes him even more attractive as a client. When I get to the lobby, I make a note of his preferences in my roster, then head home.

Chapter 6
Uncomfortable Truths

Not every city has a club devoted to kink, but thankfully, New York City does. Paddled has been around for at least twenty years, if not longer. Inside, it's anything goes, except outright sex. You can pet, fondle, kiss, whip, spank, and/or tie up. As long as all parties are consenting and everyone enjoys their play, no questions are asked.

I step into the dark space, and some of my defenses fall away. When you spend your life living on the fringe of society's preferences, it gets lonely. Here, no one asks why my preferred clothing is black patent and ties in the back. Or why I like my eyeliner dark and my lipstick intense. I can simply be.

I nod to a couple of friends as I find my way to the juice bar—some sex clubs shy away from even considering a liquor license. When you are involved in activities that involve risk and pain, you need all your wits. I order a cranberry juice and smile at the barista.

"How's it going, Tice?"

She grins back me, her beautiful face a mask of delight. "Fuckin' amazing, jelly bean. How's you?" She pumps the cranberry juice from a soda gun, looking for all the world like a real bartender.

"Not bad. Remember that business idea I talked to you about?"

"You got something for me?" Her dark eyes rake over me with intensity. Tice—also referred to as "Entice"—manages Paddled, and she's pretty confident that the owners and investors of the sex club will be interested in Kinked.

My stomach leaps into my throat. "I have a business consultant looking over it now. I can email it to you tomorrow."

"That's my girl!" She reaches over to high-five me. "Let's get this shit on the road, baby!"

I smile at her confidence. "Here's hoping your bosses like it."

She waves a hand with ridiculously long, bright blue fingernails. "I will sell that shit, baby. Don't you worry about it." She hands me my drink.

"Thanks, Tice." I've known Tice since she was a man, and I don't take her words lightly even though they're said with her flippant style. She's shrewd, and she's never been one to blow smoke.

I head for the balcony, my nerves jangling at the thought of handing over my business plan and seeing if it can finagle the financial support I'll need to get my idea off the ground. A haunting beat pumps through the space, the black walls with silver and muted magenta accents seeming to pulse with the vibe. One thing that most folks don't know about sex clubs is that you can go and just watch. Many players enjoy the taboo of onlookers, and as long as you're complimentary and not rude, your attention is often very welcome.

From my favorite perch up top, I can look down on all the activity and choose what pleasure I wish to watch. In the far corner, someone engages in rope play. A slim Asian girl closes her eyes in obvious rapture as her master ties intricate knots around her naked body. When the craft is finished, the girl has ropes pinning her arms to her sides and forming a design over her breasts and torso. The ropes are attached to the ceiling, though she isn't suspended. Her Dom draws two ends of rope between the girl's legs and begins to pleasure her.

Along the walls are alcoves with barred entrances, where people can perform a wealth of different activities. In one, a lover strikes her submissive into a frenzied orgasm using a rubber whip. Center stage is a caning already in progress. Not an activity of the faint of heart, it's the true measure of a masochist. A man lies facedown on a padded table, similar to something you might see in a massage therapy room. His wrists are bound to the head of the table, and each ankle to a corner. A long, firm rattan cane forcefully strikes his back and buttocks in measured strokes. Each hit should be separate, spaced apart, so the sub can endure the pain. A sheen of sweat covers both the sub and his Dom, and I recognize both of them. Ethan, the man tied to the table, is a long-time friend, and his Dom is his wife. It's as much work for her as a sadist as it is for Ethan, if not more so. She must watch his expressions, evaluate her pattern, make sure she gives him just enough pain, but not too much. And he can lose himself in it, focus on the bliss the pain offers, and disappear into the experience.

When they are finished, Ethan's back is covered in raw, red lines, but she did not break his skin, a true sign of a master. As he recovers, she presses a wet cloth to his face, kisses him passionately, and soon they'll disappear into the crowd, probably leave to find a private place to fuck.

I smile at their affection and remember Charles's question. Is it too much to ask to find someone who not only gets you, but is willing to give of themselves to make you happy? Don't get me wrong—I'm realistic. I know that there's no perfect match. I also recognize that I need to be with someone who understands *me*, at my core. I've dated really nice guys; I've never lasted with someone who didn't respect me. But they couldn't understand what made me tick and what turned me on after the initial novelty had passed. I don't need crazy scenes and intense setups to enjoy sex. But I do need to be in control, to be me.

Some days, I'd give anything to be "vanilla," like so many others.

I work my way through two cranberry juices before I check the time on my phone. I should head home. The confusing thoughts in my head and recent moodiness that has overtaken me are exhausting. I'm mildly distracted by a threesome setting up on the center stage: crops, clamps, and clothes pins ensuring a very intense display, but I've had enough. As I slip off my stool, I land on a foot.

"Oh, God, sorry. Are you okay?" I say as I turn to see a familiar face.

Fin smiles down at me. "Aye, it's all right. Ye're a wee thing, anyway. Hardly heavy enough to do much damage."

"What the hell are you doing here?" I ask, surprise turning to wariness.

"Lookin' for ye, as it turns out." He's dressed in jeans and a button-down shirt that hangs loose from his broad shoulders. His auburn hair curls around his collar, still damp from a recent shower, and he smells like the same yummy cologne from our last meeting, as well as fresh grass.

My throat dries out as I look up at him, the pure sexiness of him a bit overwhelming, which only serves to irritate me more. "Really? Oh,

I guess I do owe you money, come to think about it." I'd promised Stephen a cut of Ari's payment, but since he didn't show up, I hadn't sent him the cash. I create a note on my phone. "Just give me your PayPal information, and I can send it."

"Oh. Well, that's okay, then. That's not what I'm here about."

He pronounces "about" like "a-boot," and I smile despite myself. "Then what can I do for you?"

His large hand rubs the back of his neck in a familiar motion. "Aye, well, I wondered if, ye know, I could book ye?"

"Book me?" I arch an eyebrow. "For what, pray tell?"

"Weel, ye know, for services, like. Er, whatever ye call it."

Shit. The downside to not following my own rules means this guy now thinks I'm a fucking prostitute. "Yeah, well, I'm not available." I push past him, my embarrassment complete. I hear him call my name—another mistake, as all my clients know me as Mistress Hathaway, not Lux—but I keep walking. While I love a sexy high-heeled boot, you don't have the same traction as you would with, say, sneakers. I focus on the back exit that only regulars know about, and when the cool evening air hits my face, I take a deep, cleansing breath.

"Lux?"

And Scotty followed me. "Do you seriously not know when to back off? Or is being obnoxious part of your charm?"

My fury forces him back a step, his confusion evident. "I—look, I've clearly said something to upset ye, and that wasna my goal. I just wanted to see ye again, and I didn't want ye to think I was cheap. I apologize if I've offended ye."

I glare at him, but his logic seeps past my rage. "So this is you trying to ask me out?" The back alley surrounds us with cement and asphalt, our voices echoing in the cramped space.

He holds back an uncomfortable smile, looking appropriately chastised. "Aye, I guess it was, though I've made a fair mess of it." He drops his arms to his sides and blows out a breath. "Can I try again? Will ye let me, Mistress?" His eyes twinkle with renewed humor.

Those greenish blue orbs and his easy manner *are* appealing, in addition to his raw, seemingly innocent, sexiness. It doesn't hurt that I also know what he's got under those jeans, and I wouldn't mind test-driving it myself. "I'll give you one get-out-of-jail-free card. Ruin it, and there's no hope for you."

He laughs. "Fair 'nough." He sobers and meets my challenging gaze. "Mistress—Lux, rather, may I take ye to dinner?"

I'm surprised to find my mouth curving up at the invitation. And there's an odd trill in my stomach as I accept. I feel like I'm back in high school, and the guy I've had a crush on is finally looking my way.

"Friday night, then? Around seven?"

I agree to the time, as well as where to meet.

"See you then," he says as I walk away.

I turn. "Don't be late." I level my gaze at him, lips curved.

He nods, his crooked grin disarming. "Never."

Chapter 7
Second Thoughts

Dating. It's the bane of my existence. I want to skip past all the awkward glances and uncomfortable silences, weird attempts at conversation, and talking over each other accidentally…I want to hop forward to the part where you're like Ella and Ian. When they're together, they move as one. He'll sit on the couch, and she'll automatically tuck her feet against him so he can rub the arch of her foot. She's barely finished her glass of wine when he's already pouring her another. She mentions texting him, and suddenly, he's sent her some romantic, sexy message that turns her cheeks pink, even after settling into domestic monotony.

I want that. I don't want the messy, uncomfortable, unsure in-between. Alas, no one seems to have come up with a dating method that allows communication by osmosis. So I raid my closet, determined to find the right outfit.

"If I didn't know better, I'd say you were moving out," Noah comments from my doorway.

Clothing covers my bed and floor, outfits that I've either discarded or deemed ready for Goodwill. I stick my tongue out at him, then drop onto my bed, deflated. "I have a date."

He mocks shock. "What is this? The impenetrable fortress of Lux Trace has a crack?"

"Har, har."

"Aw, come here." Noah crosses the room, pulling me into a hug.

He's always warm and smelling of a spicy fragrance, and right now, it feels good to be held, though I'd never admit to it. And don't think I haven't eyed Noah a time or two for myself. I adore him. He's an incredibly giving, good-looking, and intelligent guy. Despite his rather wanton sex life, I know he's lonely and looking for the right woman. But he's a straight arrow, and I'm a labyrinthine bull's eye. We've been friends a long time; I was actually closer to him in college than I was to Ella; he and I both took business classes, while Ella took marketing and PR classes. Eventually, it all evened out, and now they are both like family to me.

I give myself the moment, then I pull free. "I can't believe I'm going to say this, but I have nothing to wear on a date with a normal guy."

He pulls out my desk chair and straddles it, resting his forearms on the back. "A normal guy? As opposed to, what? I thought Evan was pretty normal."

I dig through a mound of colors on the floor, looking for my red bra. "Evan was a submissive. He knew that about himself. This guy's… not like that."

"He's not submissive? Or he's not like Evan?"

I consider his questions as I delve into my closet again, determined to find an outfit I probably don't have. Satisfied I'm hallucinating about a patterned skirt I could have sworn I purchased, I rest a hand on my pajama-clad hip and look at Noah. "Both. Neither. I mean, he's definitely not like Evan. And he's probably not all that submissive. Which means this is going to be an utter disaster, because you kind of have to love the life in order to live with it." I hold up my pronged collar as an example of everything that won't work with this date.

"Or, it could be amazing because he's something different. You've primarily dated in the kink world so far."

I narrow my eyes at him.

"Don't give me your sexy gaze, Lulu," he teases, using a pet name he only employs when we're alone. "Think about it. You've dated how many guys in the years I've known you, all of whom knew exactly what you were about, and they've been flops. Perhaps dating someone who can be, shall we say, 'schooled' and 'trained' wouldn't be such a bad thing."

I snort. "Oh, trust me. I've tried the training bit. All I ended up with was a guy who thought I wanted threesomes every night. Which, don't get me wrong, I enjoy, but not every night."

"Oh, God, tell me you have pictures or video to show me."

I toss my pillow at him. "Don't be a guy." I lie on the bed and stare at the ceiling, its off-white surface the perfect canvas for my frustrated thoughts. "You know what I really think the problem is?"

"Hm?"

"Me."

He rests his chin on his arms. "Come on, Lux, you just haven't found the right person yet."

"Your sister said the same thing." I sigh. "And I don't know about that, Noah. I've dated men and women, lived with several, and I always leave before things get ugly. Maybe I have a commitment problem. Or maybe I'm just not cut out for long-term relationships."

Uncomfortable silence yawns between us.

"Maybe you just need to try again," he says quietly before leaving my room. "You and Ella tease me about being a love-'em-and-leave-'em, and let's face it, I can be. But I haven't given up hope. Neither should you."

Damn Noah for being a nice guy. Determined not to let tonight get to me, as it's likely one more date that will end poorly, I look for my usual wear. If any guy wants to be with me, he's going to know what he's getting.

Chapter 8

Fumbled Plans

I'm feeling slightly less confident as I approach Radio Blue in midtown. It's a novelty restaurant, which would explain why it hasn't been on my radar. Given that a horde of children just filed in, I'm not thinking this will be a romantic setting. Which is fine. It's not like I want tonight to be all hot and heavy. But I hadn't thought I'd be playing Skee-ball, either.

Besides, I'd be lying if I said I *hadn't* been reviewing the night with Ari over and over in my head. Or using Fin as a stand-in for some pretty hot daydreams. So the bright blue neon tubing and cartoon characters on the restaurant's sign are proving a bit off-putting.

Not to mention, I wore standard Lux-wear: gun-metal patent leather pants with a cobalt blue silk shell and a close-fitting, black motorcycle jacket, finished off with high-heeled ankle boots and a few silver pieces of jewelry. I went with my hair long and loose, and I toned back my makeup to a subtle eye and peachy pink lips. Tasteful? Practically virginal compared to my usual getups. For Radio Blue—which I suspect has a children's arcade in the basement—perhaps not.

He's waiting for me at the door. When he sees me, his gaze focuses on my face, for which he gets major bonus points, but his awe is evident. "Ye're stunning," he says softly, then he leans down and busses my cheek.

"You're not too bad yourself." In truth, he's stunning as well. He wears a pair of black pants that are probably part of a well-tailored suit, with a deep plum sweater that sets off the green-blue of his eyes. Given that he'd look delicious in a paper bag, I'm challenged to keep my own eyes above his shoulders.

The noise of the restaurant invades the moment as the doors open to emit a cacophony of children screaming and laughing.

"This might have been a poor choice," he comments as we walk towards the door.

"No, it's fine." I shake my head, as I don't want to make him feel bad. When we step inside, however, a "poor choice" doesn't even begin to describe it. Synthetic bleeps and loud canned music assault our ears as the bright, primary colored lights of the restaurant flicker in an array of patterns. There's a huge "exploratorium" to our left, outfitted with countless video game machines, and a restaurant with a bar upstairs. Directly behind us is a ball pit, with small children leaping through a sea of colorful plastic orbs, shrieking with delight and dismay.

The hostess wears blue furry ears and has whiskers painted on her face. "How many in your party?"

I glance at Fin, who looks supremely embarrassed.

"Should we go somewhere else?" When I say nothing, he nods. "We should. Thanks," he nods to the hostess, and then lets me lead the way out of the restaurant.

"I'm sorry," he says as we're walking out. "I feel like an ass."

I chuckle. "This doesn't bode well for the rest of the evening."

At that, he sobers. "I apologize — I dinna know—"

"No, I'm sorry. That was harsh, and I meant…it doesn't matter. I apologize." I pull together a smile. "Let's start over, shall we?"

His handsome face shows relief. "Unfortunately, I dinna know where to suggest next, not being from around here."

"I think I can come up with something. This way."

One of the benefits of living close to the city all of my life—I was born in New Jersey—is that I know a lot of people, and I'm familiar with most of the neighborhoods. I send a couple of texts while we walk to the subway stop.

Two stops later, we're above ground and stepping inside Le Chateau Lauxmont. A privately owned, chic bed and breakfast, it also houses one of the best kept secrets in the city. Once inside, you feel as though you've entered a quaint, French farmhouse, resplendent with tarnished antiques and local art. The steaks are certified Kobe, and the chef is known internationally for his skill. There's also a waiting list for Friday nights several months out, so that we are able to slip inside and get a table…let's just say, it pays to have connections.

"Shall we?" I glance at Fin, who looks appropriately impressed.

"Indeed." Fin offers me his arm, and I take it, feeling my stomach jump a little at the contact. His forearm feels like solid steel beneath my fingers. I secretly wish he would have worn short sleeves, though the cool October evening prevents that.

Once we're seated, Fin winks at me. "From now on, ye'll always choose the restaurant."

I laugh and twirl a strand of hair around my fingers. "You say that like you already know there'll be a second date."

He leans forward. "Since ye're still sitting with me after all my fuck ups so far, I'm hoping I can talk ye into it." His dimples show as he grins.

"We'll see, Fin…what is your last name?"

"MacKenzie."

"Wow. You are Scottish through and through."

"Aye. Weel, would ye expect less?"

"So, then, Mr. MacKenzie, tell me your tale." I peel off my jacket, and I notice his eyes tracing the outline of my shoulder ink.

"That's a fair piece there, and a beauty. I thought so when I first saw it, though I couldn't see it clearly. What is it, if ye don't mind me asking?"

I turn sideways so he can see the full image. "It's a peacock." The body of the bird is on my shoulder blade, and his feathers curl around my shoulder in a blaze of color.

He reaches out, his fingers trailing over the image. The touch surprises me, but he doesn't seem to have the same reticence that most people do about touch…or perhaps because I've seen him naked, the typical rules don't apply. Either way, the heat of him sends a thrill down my spine.

"That's fine work. Does it signify something for ye?"

I sit back, toying with the edge of the menu as I choose my words. "The peacock loses his feathers every year after mating season. Then, when it comes time to rustle up some female attention, he regrows them. So they've been seen as a symbol of renewal in some cultures."

His full lips quirk up at the corners. "So that's what it means to ye, then? Renewal?"

"It's like a rebirth, or being given a second chance to get it right, if you will." I narrow my eyes. "And I recognize a stall tactic when I hear one. Out with it — what's your story?"

He chuckles. "Aye, well, there's not much to tell. I'm from just outside of Edinburgh, a wee town called Kirkliston. Verra small. So when I went to university, I got see a bit of the world—at least, outside of my hometown. My da owns a small cleaners, and Mum's been working with him since they opened it. Never was much money for travel and the like, so I stayed close."

The waiter takes our drink order, and Fin waits politely until the small man leaves. "So the only real travel I ever did was playing football—well, ye call it 'soccer' here in America. I played quite a bit, and that's what I did for some time in school. Still do."

"So you're a soccer player? Er, football player, I mean?"

His cheeks pinken. "Not exactly, no. Well, I mean, aye, I do play soccer—for a local team, mind ye, not anything extravagant. I'm actually a horse trainer. Or at least, I fancy myself as such."

"Wow." I look at Fin in a new light. "That's not what I expected. I thought you were an underwear model," I tease, enjoying the flush that covers his cheeks.

"Aye, well, *that*…ye know, Stephen gets me into these things, ye understand? He told me I'd get some nice clothes out of the deal. He never mentioned I'd be photoed in my knickers."

I laugh, admittedly enjoying his discomfiture. "Stephen can definitely get you into trouble." The waiter returns with our drinks, and I take a sip of my pinot grigio. I'm anything but a wine snob, and this pinot is dry and crisp, with hints of apple. After a moment, I raise a brow and ask, "So, what did you think you were getting into last weekend?"

If he was red before, he's turned into a beet now. He covers his face with his hands, groaning comically. "Oh, God, ye had to ask. I hoped ye'd not, as I don't even have a good answer."

"Oh, come on, at least tell me what Stephen said to get you to say yes."

He digs in his pocket, coming up with his phone. "It isna what he said that sold me." He swipes over the screen, looking for something, and then hands the phone to me.

He'd pulled up his texting app.

Dude, need a favor.
I don't think u will mind helping me out.
U know the shit we talked about? I need u 2 be me. Trust me—u won't be sry.

The next text is a picture of me, though it isn't one I've seen before. I must have been at a party, and from the little bit I can tell from the background, it might be from Stephen's birthday party last year. I'm laughing, looking at the camera, and I'm wearing almost no makeup. It's the first time in a long time that I've seen myself look…well, perhaps more *me*, and less Mistress Hathaway. My gray eyes *are* mesmerizing in the photo, and though I've never seen myself as any great beauty, this photo…well, I must say, it's flattering.

Now whose cheeks are pink? I hand him the phone and finger my bread plate. "So you thought you were going to have sex with me?" I try to keep the accusatory tone out of my voice, but even so, the tension between us heightens.

"Not exactly." His burr intensifies with his chagrin. "Look, Lux, I dinna know ye, and when a friend sends me a photo of a beautiful girl and suggests I might get to see her up close…well, I dinna ask questions."

I nod, biting back a grin. "Fair enough. You do know what Stephen does, though, right?"

"Erm, I have a general idea, aye."

My estimation of him goes up. "Well, then, I'm impressed. Not every guy would jump into those shoes."

"I wasna 'jumping into his shoes.'" Fin's voice goes up a decibel. "Christ, the man will sleep with anyone for a bit of coin."

Which is true. Stephen is—technically was—an escort. He still plays that card on occasion, though most recently, he's turned his "coin" into an investment portfolio. He's part-owner of Monsieur and designs some of the fashions.

"It wasna the first time I'd seen ya, ye ken. He'd mentioned ye before. A bit of a crush he has on ye, I think." He tucks the phone away, then chances another glance at me. "So I've seen quite a few photos."

"Seriously? Like he's a total creeper?" I act more surprised than I really am. Stephen's had a thing for me for some time, and I like him. But not like that.

"I wouldna call him a 'creeper,' no, but he likes ye verra well. Listen, he sent me yer photo, and I thought if the worst thing to happen to me in New York City was that I got to bed a bonny lass, I'd be a lucky man."

I giggle, as he purposely thickens his accent, and any tension evaporates. We order dinner and chat about general things, like what brought him to the States.

"My mentor, John Littes, offered me an apprenticeship," he says between bites of steak. "Since I haven't been able to figure out what I want to do after uni, I figured I'd take him up on it."

"Are you glad you did?" I've never been close to a horse outside of stroking their satiny noses at petting zoos, so the fascination with them is curious to me.

"Och, aye. The man is a damn whisperer. He gets in the ring with them, and they immediately connect. I've never seen anything like it."

"Sounds amazing." And I mean it. While I've never been much of an animal person, his love for them is obvious. "How long are you here—in the States—for?"

"That's a good question." He pauses to chew. "I'm here on a visiting visa, but I've applied to Cornell's veterinary program so I could get a student visa. The more time I can spend learning from John, the better, and let's be honest: Cornell would be amazing." His face lights up as he talks. "I'm not sure if I'll get in, of course. It's a verra competitive field."

I am ridiculously envious of how passionate he is about his career. Didn't I used to be that way? When did I start feeling so old and afraid? When did I start coloring inside the lines so much? But then…it's been a long time since college. "Can I ask you a really personal question?"

He grins. "Ye've seen all of me there is to see. I dinna think ye can get more personal than that."

"I'll take that as a 'yes,'" I say with a chuckle. "How old are you?"

He finished chewing a bite of steak. "Does it matter?"

"Well, I'm really hoping you're old enough for that glass of wine," I say dryly.

His dimple deepens as his grin widens. "Twenty-three, if it pleases ye, Mistress."

I knew he was younger than me, but I hadn't thought he was five years younger. "Wow. Okay."

"Is it a problem for ye?"

I meet his gaze, his eyes a deep aquamarine in the low light of the restaurant. "It doesn't need to be."

Chapter 9

Dessert

It's a good date. Fun, even. Despite the awkward beginnings, I'm amazed how quickly the night flies by, even after tacking on a dessert course and coffee. And there's no lag in the conversation. Fin talks easily about his family, all of whom are in Scotland, of course, and his passion for animals. But he's also conscious to ask me questions in an attempt to draw me out. While I neatly circumvent them, I do tell him stories about strange client requests, which make him laugh.

As we leave the restaurant, he reaches for my hand, and a strange happiness curls around my core. I don't want the evening to end. The night air, while crisp, has a certain magical, romantic quality, and I go willingly when he tugs me to him. I let him guide my mouth to his; his lips are soft, but urgent, and fireworks explode over my senses. His hands slide up my back, beneath my jacket and shell, so the heat of him brands my skin.

I press into him, shifting my angle so when he opens his mouth, my tongue meets his in an erotic dance. My fingers grip his hair, my body on fire as his hands dip lower to cup my ass.

"I want to fuck you," I whisper.

He kisses me deeper, barely coming up for air until we're both breathless.

"Was that an answer?"

His forehead rests against mine. "Aye, well, I'm feeling a bit bashful. I dinna think a woman's ever said such a thing to me." His lips capture mine again in a searing kiss. "It's not like I can hide wanting ye."

I nip his lip and smile, pressing my hips against him and enjoying his groan. "Indeed. Come with me." My apartment is much too far away, and I've never been one to take someone home after a first date.

My local friendships play in my favor yet again. In this case, I know Tori, the concierge at the Hilton near Grand Central Station and my best friend in middle school. After a quick conversation, she hooks me up with a free room at a nearby Hilton. Within walking distance, soon we're in an elevator. Sadly, with other people, but that doesn't stop me from drawing his mouth down to mine.

We're both panting by the time we reach our floor, and I ignore the looks of the other passengers as we disembark and head for our room. We're barely in the door when he pulls me to him, mouth hot on my neck. The door closes of its own accord as we stumble into the interior. He lifts me, settling me around his waist, and I can feel his cock pressing against me through the layers of clothing. Definitely too much clothing.

"I want to fuck you, and in order to do that, you need to undress."

He smiles, clearly turned on by my directness. Putting me down, he removes his clothing in impressive time. I shed mine as well, down to my matching red panties and bra. He pulls a condom out of his wallet, and I nod my approval.

"Sit."

His lips twitch with amusement, but he complies. I straddle him, and he surprises me by leaning back a bit, so I don't have access to his mouth.

"Ye're beautiful, Lux, truly." He runs a finger over my collarbone, then draws it down between my breasts. "And soft." He exchanges his finger for his mouth, the heat of his breath stealing my own. He nudges my breast from its confinement, and his teeth encircle the tip, driving the edge of pain and pleasure.

When his hand travels my thigh, seeking my core, I drop my head back in anticipation, even though I haven't given an order or permission. Inside, a voice screams that I should take control back, but for the moment, as his fingers move my panties aside and tease the sensitive skin, I don't care. At some point, he removes my bra and tortures my other breast as his finger slips inside me, his thumb vibrating against my clit.

"Let me hear ye come, love," he says softly as he presses kisses against the hollow of my neck.

I nearly come apart with my orgasm, the sensation breaking over my skin like needles of pleasure. I grip his shoulders as he doesn't let up, forcing me into an even greater high as another wave rocks my core.

Curled against him, I try to get my bearing once my breath stabilizes. His arms surround me, his fingers stroking my skin. I'm out of my element, confused by how intense the experience was, so I fill the moment with my mouth on his, my hands deep in his hair, gripping. He submits easily, even when I push him down to the bed, grinding against his hard cock, satin panties all that separate us. I devour his lips, stopping only to reach for the condom and remove my panties. I feather my fingers over his sensitive underside, admiring the size of him.

He grips the sheets. "Jesus," he exhales as I bend close to his cock, blowing gently over the silken skin.

I slide down on him, my hyper-sensitive nerve endings colliding as his cock fills me. He sucks in a breath, eyes closed, as I gently rock my hips, easing his full length inside. Containing my response becomes challenging as he grips my hips, so I lace my fingers through his and confine them above his head. He tries to kiss me, but I hover over him, my hair creating a veil around his face. I meet his gaze with a challenge in my own. As though understanding my desire without a word, he begins to thrust deep, the size of him stretching me as the delicious friction increases. A moan escapes my control, and I have to close my eyes as expanding sensations overwhelm me.

My hands tighten around his, and I meet his rhythm with my own until the explosion of pleasure destroys all attempts at restraint. He quakes beneath me moments later, groaning into my hair. I collapse beside him, both of us spent.

"So, that was…something."

We're lying in bed, doing something I rarely do: cuddle. Or at least, I struggle with it, because it doesn't come easily to me. In this man's arms, it feels…good. Perhaps even right, though I'd be hard-pressed to say that out loud. I've just met him, after all, and there's every chance he'll head home, and I'll never see him again.

I brush a finger over the light smattering of ginger-colored curls across his chest. "Aye, it was." I try to mimic his accent, but it's a horrible attempt, and we both end up laughing.

"Can I ask ye something personal?"

I turn onto my stomach, and his arm follows, his fingers finding the back of my neck and kneading my scalp. I could purr, it feels so amazing. "Turnabout is fair play, and if you keep that up, I'll tell you anything." I stretch my head forward so he has better access. "What did you want to ask?"

It takes him a moment before he responds. "Is it always like that for ye? I mean, when you are working, that is? With Ari, it seemed like ye really enjoyed it, I mean."

Inwardly, I cringe. *This is why you have rules, Lux. And this is what happens when you break them.* I roll over, away from his touch, and look for my underwear. Spying them on the floor, I get up. As I dress, he watches me, face cautiously blank.

"I dinna mean to offend ye."

I stop, silk tank in place, holding my pants in one hand. "You didn't. This isn't your fault. It's mine." I stare at the wall to gather my words. "I don't usually sleep with clients. I'm a professional Dominatrix, not a prostitute. The other night with Ari…she's a friend." Lying is easier than trying to explain all the times I've broken the rules over the last few months. "Most of what I do is to help others have their fantasies, but I don't get involved sexually."

"So," his brows draw together, "Professional Dominatrices dinna have sex with their clients? So what is it ye do then? Not meaning to sound daft, but I can't say I'm all that familiar with the profession."

His question and tone of voice are so innocent, I chuckle. "Honestly, that's a good question. What do I do? Let's see… I work with people who have fetishes or want to be dominated. Or they might be like Ari, and not really know what they want, so I help them sort that out."

"Aye, well, I imagined that well enough. But how do you do that *without* having sex with them?" He shifts to his side so he can look at me, and I can't help but admire the muscular curves of his shoulders.

I shrug. "I do what they like, and that's all they pay me for."

"Aren't they a bit aroused after ye're done?"

"Yeah, usually. That's for them to take care of." I can't believe I'm actually blushing. But his intense curiosity and rapt attention feel different. Most people are either put off by what I do or make crude comments. So his honest questions are a change. Or maybe it's that he's gorgeous and naked. That could be it too, I suppose.

"Damn, woman. Ye're cruel."

I wink. "Of course. That's what they pay me for."

"So… could ye show me what ye do for a client sometime? Though I'd like to keep with the fucking part after, if ye don't mind."

I've changed my mind on getting dressed, given that he's, well, delicious. I drop a knee onto the bed. "Mr. MacKenzie, do you wish to be tortured? Is that what you're saying?" I slink onto all fours on the mattress.

He has the good sense to look confused. "Aye, well, I dinna mean I want ye to abuse me, Mistress." He watches me circumspectly as I move towards him. "But I wouldna mind experiencing bits of it."

"I'll have to see what I can do." And then I kiss him. He stretches out beside me, pulling me against him, and I lose myself in his scent and touch. He manages to remove the clothing I hastily donned, and desire burns a path across my skin as he aligns my body with his. Spreading my legs so he can rub himself against me, he reaches down over my ass and slides his fingers along my already wet sex. I wrap my leg around his hip, giving him easier access. When his fingers slip inside me, I hold him to me, unable to stop the climax that builds. But my arm is trapped beneath us, and even as I reach my crescendo, panic builds in its wake. His mouth drowns out the scream that threatens.

Several moments pass before he realizes that I'm crying, and if I hadn't just had an orgasm that left my legs weak, I would move away. Instead, I try to hold in the wails that fight for escape. I wriggle to get my arm free, and he shifts back, giving me enough space to do so.

"Jesus, Lux, what happened? Did I hurt ye? What is it?"

When I don't respond—can't—he wraps himself around me, pulling me on top of him as I battle with an inner demon that I refuse to let win. He strokes my hair and shoulders, whispering nonsensical words that are oddly comforting in his deep voice.

And then I fall asleep, victorious over the dark.

Chapter 10
Good News

There is nothing more embarrassing than crying after sex. Okay, there probably is. But in my small corner of the world, that's pretty much the worst. And of course, Fin only wanted to know how he could help. This morning. Because not only did we have sex on the first date—which is not an unusual thing for me—but we also slept through the night—which is highly unusual for me. And there's nothing worse than dressing in the same clothes from the night before. Bleck.

Nonetheless, I learn three things about Fin as a result. One, he is adorable in the morning. Like he's seriously one of those guys that wakes up warm, handsome, and delicious. I know—hate him, right? Except that there's the second thing I discovered, which is that he's even more amazing in bed the next day. And three, he's a ridiculously sweet guy. Perhaps even a good guy. And he wouldn't say good-bye this morning until I assured him that last night's emotional brouhaha had nothing to do with him, was a result of being exhausted, and I would be fine.

Which causes me all kinds of concern on the subway ride home because I ruin good guys. Or at least, I ruin relationships with good guys. Despite my best attempts in the past, I've never been able to get things to last, and if I'm honest, it's my issue. Or issues...

When I get home, all I can think about is Fin's parting kiss, the last taste of his skin, and the final touch of his hand on the back of my neck.

Fuck.

I do not have time for this. Or the emotional bandwidth. Or… whatever. I just don't. And when I walk in the door, Noah is already on the case.

"Wow. That was either a very high-paying client, or someone got fucked good last night." He raises an appraising eyebrow and circles me. "Hm, I'm going with a good fucking. Anyone I know? Or should know?"

I give him a withering glance, uncomfortable with his harmless insinuation that cuts just a bit too close. "Given all the times you come in with rumpled clothes and I don't give you shit, I should get a pass."

He clucks. "Now, Lulu, don't get all pissy. I know the walk of shame when I see it. And darlin', you got the swagger."

I head for the coffee, thankful he left a bit of tar behind. I make a face and dump cream in the sludge to make it palatable, then swallow it down. Noah joins me in the kitchen and gestures to the morning paper, but right now, it doesn't appeal.

"I'm going to get a shower."

His clever eyes miss nothing. "Damn, Lux…you got it bad for this one. It's written all over you. And you won't talk about it, which means he's either a client, which is a no-no, or someone new you don't want me to know." He taps a finger against his lips. "Interesting."

I heave a sigh. "I will deal with you after I feel human. And you stop annoying me."

But even the heavy blast of the shower head doesn't wash away the doubts and fears coursing through my mind. Or Fin's scent.

"Are you going to see him again?"

Noah's made a fresh pot of coffee, which went a long way to earning him my good graces. I gave him the short version of last night and this morning, though I omit the crying part. "God, like I have an answer for that."

"Perhaps the better question is, *when* are you going to see him again? Because he's clearly under your skin, Lulu, my pet, and you've got it bad. I don't think even Evan had you this turned around."

I stick my tongue out at him even though he's right. I really liked Evan. Fin…he's something different.

My phone rings, and I pull it out of my jeans pocket. "Hello?"

"You ready to get into business, baby?"

"Tice?" I'd know her voice anywhere. And what did she just say? "Are you serious?"

"Fuck yeah, I'm serious. They love it. In fact, they don't just love it, they think it's brilliant. They want in, and they don't want you to look anywhere else. Look for a call from Divine Incorporated later this week."

"Oh my God."

"I sold you like you shit fourteen karat gold, baby. Breathe it in, and let it be. Gotta rock, but I had to call you as soon as I heard."

I say goodbye, then stare at Noah.

"You either got really good news or the worst news ever, judging by the way your hands are shaking." He reaches across the table, his fingers warm against my cold ones. "You okay?"

"Divine Incorporated wants to back Kinked. Like, completely. They're in."

"That's fantastic!" He pulls me out of my chair and hugs me, lifting me up off my feet.

Still in disbelief, I hug him back. "This is really happening, right?"

He grabs my face, kisses my forehead, and looks into my eyes with his intense baby blues. "Of course it is. I told you this idea was brilliant. Now you get to do the really hard work—make it happen."

I force myself to take a deep breath. "I can't believe it. That was too easy."

"Yeah, well, the rest of it won't be so easy, so enjoy the one part of it that was."

"Right. Yes. Shit." I don't even know what to say or think.

My phone vibrates on the table.

Had an amazing night…and morning. When can I see you again?

If my insides weren't already jelly, they would be now. I hand it to Noah. "Answer for me."

He looks down at the phone, then at me. "It's the boy toy. You sure?"

I don't answer, just look at him, and he obliges. Then he stands and stretches, kisses me on top of my head, and tucks my phone back in my hand. "I have to get going—big dinner party tonight, and I think Ella mentioned elephants and trick ponies being involved."

"Sounds like my kind of evening."

He chuckles. "Could be. And congrats, Lux. This is going to

work—I have a good feeling about all of it. And I'm never wrong." I wave as he heads for the door. Then I glance at my phone to see what Noah typed in.

How about tonight?

Gee, Noah, thanks.

This time, we decide on pizza. And we order in. After all, I spent the night with the guy. It seems a bit prudish not to invite him to my house at this point. Not to mention, I want to enjoy his body again, and I can't keep calling in favors.

Fin insists on having a drink to toast my good news.

"I'm very happy for ye." He watches me as we each take a sip, and when I put my glass down, he pulls me to him, his lips tasting of wine and cinnamon. "So, does this mean I'll have to create an online persona to get a date with ye? I'm not much for social media."

"A curmudgeon?"

He makes a face, causing me to giggle. "Aye, the whole 'smart phone' bit and Facetube and YouBook—my mates are all crazy over it. I dinna care for any of it."

"Wow. You are really are a die-hard for the olden days, eh?" I kiss him so he can't respond. "And that's *Facebook* and *YouTube*. And you aren't seeing anyone or doing anything unless it's 'Facebook official,' so…" I enjoy the feel of his five o'clock shadow against my fingertip as I trace his jaw.

He snorts. "Aye, well, I'm just as happy being 'unofficial.'" His lips find mine. "Much more clandestine that way."

I slip my arms around his waist, relishing the feel of him against me. "Terrified of social media, hm? Any other fears I should be aware of? Spiders? Corporate greed?"

"Spiders, no. Corporate greed…isn't everyone? How about ye, Lux Trace? What's yer deepest fear?"

While several things come to mind, I go with the safest answer. "Flying." I shudder. "I absolutely hate being airborne."

"Really? Why?"

I consider his question. "I'm not sure. Something about being up there, knowing that if something happens, you have no control over any of it. Yeah, I do *not* fly. I'll drive just about anywhere. Love trains. But I will do quite a bit to avoid flying."

"A Dominatrix who doesn't like being out of control on a plane." He grins. "Somehow, I'm not surprised."

I laugh, lead him to the living room, and push him down onto the couch.

"So, when do I get full Mistress Hathaway treatment?" he asks as I straddle him, enjoying the play of his muscles under my hands as he shifts to accommodate me. We're both in jeans and t-shirts, but that won't last for long.

We kiss, and for a long while, the focus of his mouth on mine distracts me completely. Eventually, I pull back and look at him. "You don't know anything about BDSM, do you?"

"I've heard of it, of course, and I have a general idea—particularly after being in Paddled—but no, not other than that. Is that a problem? I dinna mind that you like it."

I roll my eyes. "Famous last words."

"Why?"

He seems genuinely curious about my reaction, so I try to boil it down for him. "It's hard to maintain a relationship when you don't have common interests. Don't get me wrong—I enjoyed last night. And I'm sure I'll enjoy tonight," I outline his bottom lip lightly with my finger. "But BDSM is a preference. A taste, if you will. It's like trying to eat frozen yogurt to satisfy you, when all you really want is gelato."

His hands slide up my arms, giving me a pleasant chill as he mulls over my words. "I much prefer gelato," he says with a grin. "So, would I know if I like it? I mean, are ye born that way? Or is it more of an…"

"Acquired taste? That's a good question. Sometimes it's a bit of both." I pause, giving his comment some thought. "I've had clients who've always known what they like. Some know, but they haven't felt free to express it. Others…they struggle finding what they enjoy. Like Ari. She knew she wanted to submit, but she was scared to do it again, because it's been used against her by previous partners."

He shakes his head. "That's too bad. She seemed verra sweet and gentle."

"She is. And a very good person. I'm glad I could help her find that safe place to be herself again."

After a few more moments of consideration, he nods, as though coming to a decision. "Should we try it then? Will ye show me what I've been missing out on?"

I silence him with my mouth, unsure how to answer him. I've never been in this position before, as someone's *first* foray in BDSM. I've always been drawn to—or sought out by—people already in the community. They might not have been active or clear on their preferences, but they already had a solid handle on whether they liked it or not. "You really want to try it out?"

He grins, making him even more delicious. "Weel, I think I do. Maybe I only want to see a wee bit of what ye do. Get my feet wet, ye ken?"

I sit back, grinning in return. "Did a little bit of research, did you?"

"Aye, and there's some scary shite out there. Do ye really abuse a man with a bullwhip? Beat him with bare fists? And use clothespins on his balls?" His quirked eyebrow tells me exactly how he feels about that.

"Mmm." I lean down and press my lips against the blade of his jaw, nudging his head over so I have access to his neck. "*Aye*, I have."

"And they wanted ye to do that, then?"

I trace the vulnerable curve of his neck, catching his skin between my teeth in light nips. "They paid me to do it."

He snorts derisively. "I dinna think I could take such things on my balls. Of course, I dinna think I would like being beaten on, either, with whips or fists, ye ken."

His accent makes his insistence even more entertaining. I lose track of my sensual plan and end up with my head against his shoulder, hiccupping with laughter. "Oh my God," I breathe, trying to recapture my composure. "You make it awfully hard to give you the 'full treatment' when you don't like any of my specialties." When his eyes widen, I fall back into giggles. "I'm kidding! God, I can't breathe." I wave my hands in front of my face, in an effort to…well, hell, I'm not sure why I do it, but it seems to help. I flop beside him, then glance up at him. "Oy. I haven't laughed like that in a long time."

"I'm glad to amuse you," he says wryly. Then he smiles and kisses me, nearly taking my breath away again.

I push him back. "I don't get involved in anything involving beatings or bullwhips, but I have used a clothespin or two in my time." I wink. "How about this: we'll play with a little bondage—no pain—and see how you like it? That will give you an opportunity to tell me what you think." I place a hand on his chest, holding him back from kissing me again. "And listen—don't say you like something if you don't, just to make me happy. This is supposed to be fun and sexy for both parties."

He lifts my hand from his chest, then kisses my fingertips before pressing his lips against my palm. "I promise."

Chapter 11

Kinked

I don't invite a lot of people into my bedroom. As a result, I tend to have clothing all over the place and various personal care products spread out over my dresser. So I barely recognize my own room. I'd picked up and put away everything, vacuumed and dusted and organized every corner, and generally recreated the entire space in the hours before Fin arrived.

I'd also set it up *just in case* he wanted to play. Hey, a girl can hope, can't she? Our earlier conversation was wildly convenient for my hopes for tonight. I light the candles I've strategically placed around the room. True to my ink, I'm a fan of peacocks, so my room's theme reflects as much in small accents.

He eyes the neatly made bed and firelight. "Either ye are verra perceptive, or I'm a suckling pig to slaughter."

"I wasn't even a Girl Scout," I tease, but when he looks confused, I shake my head. "Never mind. I try to be prepared for every eventuality." Something about this man makes me want to smile whenever I look at him, but I can't analyze that too closely right now. Or ever, really. I sober, forcing myself into seriousness. "For the next hour, you will refer to me as Mistress or Mistress Hathaway. If I tell you to do something, you do it. Understood?"

My change of persona surprises him, but a slow grin spreads across his face. "Yes, Mistress."

God, he is beautiful. I fight to keep from smiling in return. "If I do anything that you don't like, you will tell me."

"Should we have a safe word?"

I drop the facade for a moment. "No. We aren't doing anything involving pain, and all you have to do is say something."

"All right then."

With a deep breath, I close my eyes, centering my thoughts and returning to Dom mode. "Take off your clothes. I want to see you."

He complies, watching me while he does so. He pauses when he's only in bikini briefs—which I recognize from the billboard. "Did you want me to take—"

"Did you not understand me?" I snap the words, eyes challenging.

He doesn't look away, but instead meets my gaze as he removes his briefs. The intensity between us gives me a thrill, as a true submissive would break contact. I've never worked with someone who challenged me, and I'm surprised by how my stomach leaps with excitement.

He stands straight, unnervingly calm. And looking like my very own Greek god with his pale skin and muscled body. I swallow hard, resisting the impulse to break form and throw him on the bed now and have my way with him.

I swallow against the dry patch in my throat, then make an act of appraising him. He closes his eyes as I trail a hand down his arm, then follow a path across his flat stomach, within an inch of his erection. I walk a circle around him, enjoying his perfect stillness, the way the candlelight plays over the planes and hollows of his skin. I keep him off balance with light touches and pause to enjoy the perfection that is his ass. Trust me—it's worthy of worship. He starts when I press a kiss to his smooth back, unable to resist.

I return to face him, and his eyes are closed, his mouth relaxed. Dear God. I have to mentally smack myself to stay focused.

"Lie down on the bed."

He obeys, and I reach for the ties that are always at the four corners of my queen-size bed. They are soft black rope, easily knotted and released, and I bind all four limbs. Then I stand back to examine my handiwork. There is nothing quite like a gorgeous man bound. Particularly Fin. He has his eyes closed again, breathes steadily, and even when I move around the room, he doesn't twitch. I strip out of my clothing, leaving my black satin bra and g-string in place.

When I settle onto the mattress, he turns his head towards me with a lazy smile, admiring my body. "If this is as bad as it gets, I think I'll be fine."

I offer him a deadpan expression, but inside, I might have melted a bit. Nonetheless, I hold up a crop, its leather end soft as butter from years of use. "If you were a client, I'd start with this." I drag the soft leather along his torso.

He drops his head back to the pillow, steeling himself against laughing. "That tickles."

"It wouldn't if I was using it properly."

"Aye, well…where would ye normally apply it?"

"Back of the legs," I say, slapping the top of his thigh lightly. "Ass. Back." Very lightly, I tap it against his straining length. "Cock."

He blows out a breath. "I think I'll skip the flagellation, if that's okay with ye, Mistress."

I chuckle, despite my determination to stay in character. "We're playing, Fin. I'm not going to hurt you," I raise an eyebrow, "yet."

Tucking the crop behind me, I reveal a lone peacock feather.

He grins. "Aye, ye're definitely going easy on me."

"You say that now." I smirk, then lay the feather lightly against his skin.

He shivers, pulling against the restraints. "Ye might have a point."

I tease him, dragging the light fringe over his shoulders, his forearm, and taking an agonizingly slow route to his cock. He tries to stay still, but between the tickling plume and the super sensitive areas, he struggles between laughter and sighs of pleasure.

When I swirl the feather over his swollen head, he exhales heavily, fighting a smile of pleasure.

"How does that feel?"

He opens his mouth to answer, but I don't let up. Pulling hard against the ropes, his back arches.

"It seems I might have found your poison."

I torture him a bit more, enjoying his inability to hold still, before I abandon the feather in favor of more involved pleasures. He watches me, and I find myself reveling in his appreciation of my body. I uncurl slowly, then settle between his legs. When my fingers follow the curve of his thick cock, my bed shakes with his strain.

"God, Lux, ye're killin' me."

"I'm sorry—who are you speaking to?" I withdraw my touch.

His gaze centers on me as he spits out through gritted teeth. "*Mistress.*"

I bite back my grin and don't respond, but continue the agonizingly slow caress, until I take him in my mouth. Flicking my tongue against his aroused skin, his hips shift with my rhythm. Between his width and length, I can't take him all in, but he groans when he presses against the back of my throat.

When he's shaking with need, I withdraw, sitting back on my heels.

He opens one eye. "Goddamn ye, woman. Untie me."

I offer him a sly smile. "That's not how this works, Mr. MacKenzie. First, you never address me without saying 'please.' And second," I stretch myself over him, trapping his cock as I sit astride him. "I'm not finished."

He tenses his shoulders, his head falling back. "Ye're evil." Then he lifts his head up briefly. "*Mistress.*"

I laugh, then remove my bra and bend over him, offering him my nipple. "You have no idea just how evil I can be."

He suckles me eagerly, and I'm so aroused from our play that I'm not sure how much longer *I* can hold out. I breathe deeply, lose myself in the moment, feeling a spreading warmth from my center expand over my thighs. His teeth close on the tip of my breast, the pain warring against the exquisite pleasure.

When I finally mount him, we're both nearly begging, and I'm so wet I take him in nearly to the hilt. I ride him mercilessly, knowing he is unable to thrust fully into me, and the intensity seems endless as I lean forward, pressing my breasts against him as I savage his mouth. He quakes against me, and when I sense he's close to the brink, I let myself go, falling over the edge with abandon. He goes with me, mouth desperate against mine, as we plunge into sensation.

Afterwards, I untie him, and he shakes his hands and legs to get back his circulation. I'm about to ask how it was, but he reaches for me, pulling me into his lap and devouring my mouth. I'm breathless when he finally pulls away.

"You are incredible."

I preen under his compliment. "I can be. I take it you liked it?"

"Verra much. When's it my turn?"

"What do you mean?"

"When do I get to tie ye up and torture ye? Seems only fair."

I laugh. "Uh, no."

He leans back on the bed, propping himself up on one arm. "Why not?" He asks it without menace, but my hackles go up regardless.

"Because I'm a dominant woman, and I'm like that in the bedroom one hundred percent of the time." I wriggle off the bed, putting away my tools, which conveniently ensures I don't have to look at him. *This is why you don't take on newbies*, I chide myself harshly. *So you don't have to deal with these kinds of questions.* If I'm being honest—what is that I hear? My conscience laughing at me?—there's more to it than my protests... though I barely admit it to myself. The air has cooled, causing goosebumps on my naked skin.

I'm vaguely aware of his movements, but it still takes me a little off guard when he slides his hands around my waist, gently nudging me back against him. His body radiates heat, and he eases my slight chill. "Have ye never tried?" His breath brushes against my ear, his voice soft.

I would prefer not to answer, but he's been nothing but honest and accepting so far. I let down my guard a hair. "No, I haven't. I know I wouldn't like it," I say in a low tone.

He holds me, rests his chin against the top of my head. "If ye'd ever be up to the challenge, I'd love to see ye just as I was, spread wide and naked." His hand trails down, finding just the right spot between my legs where I'm still taut from orgasm. "I'd love to push my cock into ye, feel yer liquid heat, knowing ye could do nothing more than lie back and enjoy." He turns me and kneels down. "And I'd use my mouth on ye, love." He spreads my legs, and I lean back against the footboard of the bed. "Giving ye pleasure ye'd be unable to refuse." His hot tongue finds me immediately, his fingers plunging deep inside me. He slides my thigh over his shoulder, giving him even greater access as he slides yet another finger into the rhythm. The fullness is so incredible, and I can't stop the cries of pleasure from echoing in the room as he laves my clit. My fingers sink into his hair, holding him against me as my release grips me and fireworks explode behind my eyelids.

I sag against the bed, spent, and he returns to his feet, taking me back into his arms. "Do ye think ye might be willing to let me try? I think ye might enjoy it more than ye think."

And I'm shocked to hear myself say: "I'll think about it."

Chapter 12

Divine Accommodations

A week later, Noah and I meet Ella and Ian at our favorite restaurant in the Village: a small Italian dive that has the best marsala you'll ever taste. Fin had to work late tonight, and I was caught between sad and thankful. We've seen each other almost every night, and while it's taking a toll on our sleep patterns—particularly his, as he has to be at a barn twenty miles outside the city by six a.m. to start work—we haven't minded. While I want to introduce him to my friends, there's a part of me that likes having this separate part of my life that is just me.

Ella, who usually glows despite exhaustion, has circles under her eyes. Ian hovers over her a bit, and I eye her closely. "Are you getting sick?"

She shakes her head, then leans against Ian's solid shoulder. "No, I'm just beat. We've had what—four? Five?—parties in the last three days. Between that, my baby who depends on me for sustenance 24/7, and his stepdad's heart attack, it's been a week."

"Wait, what happened to your stepdad?" I look at Ian. Always handsome and elegant, even his usual easy smile seems to have a few cracks around the edges.

"It happened two days ago. He'll be fine, as it was minor with no permanent damage. He's been working too hard, as we've all been telling him. But he doesn't listen. This was his wakeup call." He rubs the back of Ella's neck as she turns her face towards him for a kiss.

"I'm so sorry—that had to be terrifying."

He sighs. "It was, but he's going to be okay."

I nod, but I'm surprised Ella didn't tell me.

Even tired, she senses my question. "I barely had time to get to the hospital in between parties and the kids."

"It's okay. I can see you're beat. You know I can help if you need anything."

She laughs. "Right, between whipping asses and the new man on the scene? Where would you have time?" She raises an eyebrow at me.

"I always make time for my friends." My cheeks warm. "I see someone's been telling tales." I glare at Noah.

Noah holds up his hands. "You never said I couldn't tell her about the new sexy on your whipping post."

I roll my eyes and chuckle. "Sexy is right." I look at Ella. "He's the guy on that billboard in Times Square for Monsieur."

Her mouth forms an "O" of surprise. "You mean the hot redhead with the fabulous ass?"

Ian smirks at Noah. "And they say we men are terrible."

Noah smiles. "I've lived with both of them. I can assure you that they are both just as bad as, if not worse than, us."

I snort. "Whatever, Mr. I-Date-at-Least-Four-Women-a-Month."

"'Date' is such a misleading word."

I nearly spit out my vodka and soda. "At least you're honest."

Ella clears her throat loudly. "Back to the *important* subject at hand: so tell me more. Name, age, height, pedigree?"

"Fin; twenty-three; six-four, maybe? And he's Scottish, a 'footballer,' currently interning as a horse trainer, and wants to study to be a veterinarian."

She whistles softly. "Wow. I'd definitely have me some of that, t'were I in your position. And he's younger, eh? Better stamina."

I nod as Ian laughs. "You are incorrigible, Mrs. Cane."

"Hm. We'll see how incorrigible you think I am later tonight," she teases as her arm moves beneath the table.

"Hey, you two. Get. A. Room. I'm the baby here, and you might ruin my innocence." Noah holds his napkin over his eyes.

"Younger by two freakin' months," I point out as we're both twenty-eight, but at this point, we're all laughing.

Noah gives me a pointed look. "Are you going to tell them your other awesome news?"

Ella's eyes light up as she and Ian look expectantly at me.

I wasn't keeping it a secret, but I wasn't sure if I was ready to admit it was real, either. So I inhale deeply before the words tumble out. "Well, it was rumor up until today. But I got the official word from Divine, Inc. earlier today—they own Paddled as well as a couple of sex clubs in L.A. and Chicago," I explain as my stomach jumps at the idea of saying my news out loud, "they want to invest in Kinked."

"Congratulations!" Ella jumps out of her chair to hug me. "This is so awesome! I told you it would rock."

Ian embraces me as well. "Very happy for you, Lux."

Once again seated, Ella digs out her phone. "My best friend, entrepreneur, and business owner of the hottest new international dating site…smile for the camera, Ms. Trace."

I make a fish face, and she snaps the photo.

"This calls for champagne." Ian signals the waiter, and within minutes, we're toasting.

"To your hard work and success," Noah says, and we all join in with "salute" and clink glasses.

As I sip the sharp, fruity champagne, two emotions race though my veins: giddy excitement and jittery fear. But for once, the excitement is stronger.

Ella meets my gaze across the table, her smile of pride a boon to my nerves. "You're going to rock this, lady."

I nod and hold my glass out to hers again. "Agreed."

The downside to getting investors? Shit gets real.

For the next two days, I spend day and night with Noah, fine-tuning my business plan in order to submit a final version to Divine, Inc.'s accounting and marketing departments, as well as to the CEO. I advertise on freelance and free posting sites for coding and website experts, graphic designers, and internet dating consultants.

"How are you going to pay for this?" Noah asks as I receive responses to my ads and price quotes.

"Since I don't yet have any paperwork from Divine, with my savings. Do you mind if I don't pay the rent for the next six months?" I tease.

He grins. "I can take out your rent in other ways."

"Hm." I look at him appraisingly. "I can totally whip your ass and have you begging for release in five minutes flat."

With a laugh, he nods. "You'd definitely have me begging—for you to stop." He shivers. "I'm definitely not into pain."

"Don't knock it 'til you try it, Storm."

He looks mildly afraid, but then he sobers. "Lux, if you need to skip a few month's rent, that's fine. Seriously. I can pay for everything on my own."

I shake my head. "No. I'll figure it out. But thanks."

The cost estimates are broad, ranging from ouch to yowie, and I'm not even sure I know what to look for, but I parse out the information, using my knowledge of spreadsheets gleaned from a few years as an account manager before my Dominatrix days.

By the end of the next week, I've interviewed and selected a handful of designers and coders to work on the website, and I've got meetings scheduled for the next three months with Divine, Inc.'s marketing team. I make an appointment with Divine's project manager for Kinked to sign the final paperwork. I should be elated. And I am…mostly. But there's still a part of me that cautions: *you've never done anything like this. You could be a total failure. Who do you think you are, to take on a project this large, interfere with the love lives of people, and then expect to make a living?*

I try to ignore it, to push away the negative thoughts, but I'd be lying if I said I was confident. I want this. I do. But what if I fail?

Fin asks me out for, of all things, bowling. I've long since clipped my nails short, as any amount of computer work puts a stop to my sexy, long nails. It doesn't matter, though—I'm a horrible bowler. Fin refuses to believe me until after our first game where I can count more gutter balls than points.

"Ye're terrible," he finally agrees in disbelief.

I sit back in the molded chair, grinning. "Told you. Worst. Bowler. Evah." I own the title quite happily.

"Do ye want me to help ye a bit?" He's so baffled by my complete inability, he stares at me in awe.

"Nope. I'm not that into it. But I'm happy to let you whip my ass… here." I wink and take a sip of my soda.

He reaches for my hands, pulling me to my feet and kissing me soundly. "Aye. But I'd rather do it elsewhere," he teases.

How on earth is this turning me on? Yet it is, and I refuse to contemplate it further. "Keep dreaming, MacKenzie." I punctuate my response by nibbling his bottom lip, then tracing it with my tongue.

When we finally separate, he clears his throat. "Well, I've no wish to keep beating ye *here*. What else would ye like to do?"

We're both dressed casually, and my jeans are getting more wear than typical. I'm also saving on makeup costs, as I enjoy being a bit more bare-faced around Fin. There's something about him that puts me at ease, and I don't mind looking younger and less edgy. Usually I hate that I look barely legal—hard to garner much respect that way. With Fin…it's different. He makes me feel like it doesn't matter. Which brings up all sorts of uncomfortable questions that I don't want to deal with.

"We could go home and find fun things to do." I link my hands behind his neck. "We can even stop by the sex shop on our way back to see if we find something fun to enjoy."

His eyes widen. "A sex shop? I canna say I've ever been to one."

I lean back in his arms, face to the ceiling. "You are such an innocent!" Then I smile at him. "I feel like I'm Mrs. Robinson, debauching her young lover."

"I'm willing to be corrupted, Mistress." He nuzzles my neck, finding the spot to nip with his teeth that sends my hormones soaring.

"Then I shall lead on, my little lamb. Into the lion's den we go."

Shay's Sexy Suite is anything but a lion's den. Fashionably decorated with soft, reddish pink chintz and white velvet, it screams girly good times, rather than sexual depravity. Shay burns a light incense in the back, which, when combined with whatever strawberry fragrance she uses out front, creates a welcoming patina for the senses. Fin is, as usual, completely at ease, his fascination with the array of elegant toys on display refreshing. Hell, I could just watch him walk around the room and get turned on.

In the "back room," the decor turns dark and moody, but still with a feminine vibe. Here, Shay sells the heavier sex items, like expert canes and whips that are hand-crafted by artisans from all over the world. Fin loses himself in examination of crops, and I wander over to the leatherwear.

When I feel a light hand on my shoulder, I turn in surprise.

"Mistress Hathaway!" Ari practically leaps into my arms with enthusiasm. "So good to see you." She busses my cheek lightly, then steps back in sudden shyness. "This is my friend, Bryant."

A dark-haired man steps up beside her, built nearly as petite as she is, though he stands a head taller than her. "Nice to meet you, Mistress. Ari's told me a lot about you."

I take his hand in a firm shake. "Good to meet you as well." Ari's glowing with happiness, and Bryant seems smitten. "You look happy, my dear. I'm glad to see it."

"Oh, I *so* am. Thanks to you." Her light skin flushes, and she glances over when Fin approaches. "Oh, wow. Hi! I didn't know you two were a couple."

Ah, the moment of truth. "Fin, you remember Ari, I'm sure. Bryant, Fin."

The difference between the two men is particularly obvious as Bryant's slim hand gets lost in Fin's. If Bryant knows who Fin is, or how recently he had sex with Ari, he doesn't let on.

We engage in the requisite small talk, but Ari and Bryant are clearly into each other and want to get going. Ari follows Bryant out after we've said goodbye, but after a moment, she returns and pulls me aside.

"Bryant is nothing like the guys I told you about before. I've known him for years, but I never had the guts to act on his interest." She hugs me again. "Thank you so much." Her eyes shine with joy.

I drop a kiss on her forehead. "You are very welcome. I'm glad you're happy. He seems like a keeper."

She nods, then casts a sly glance over at Fin. "So does he. I'm happy for you, too."

We exchange grins, and my heart feels lighter as I watch her nearly skip out of the room towards her lover. I slip behind Fin and thread my arms around his waist. "Watch'ya looking at?" I peer around his shoulder.

He's handling a rubber flogger handmade from recycled bike tires, according to the description on the price tag. I crane my neck to see his expression, amused when I discover something between horror and fascination there.

"You thinking you'd like to give that a whirl?" I tease.

He doesn't say anything, just lays it back out on its display pad. His arm circles my waist, drawing me against his side, and then he whispers, "I'd be begging for death."

I laugh. "Only if your lover doesn't do it right. It's not as bad as it looks." I glance back at the flogger. "Well, maybe that one is. But we'll stick with the fun stuff." I wink at him, and we return to the front.

Shay is dusting the front counter, looking nothing like a sex shop owner.

"Lux Trace? Girl, get over here and give me a squeeze!"

I gladly follow instructions, as Shay is a dear friend. Tall, with plenty of curves, her mixed ethnic background reads like a Who's Who of the Middle East. As a single mom with three kids, she's always been tough as nails, but she's well known in the kink and vanilla communities alike as someone who makes it comfortable for just about anybody to buy something to amp up their sex life.

I introduce Fin, and she gives me a knowing grin. "Uh-huh. So you're looking for a little something to spice up the night?"

Fin turns an attractive shade of pink. "What would ye recommend?"

"I recommend you keep talking, gorgeous. Damn, girl, how do you stand it? With that sexy accent and that smile—not to mention those eyes—you just come with me, honey. We'll see who you go home with tonight." She grins as only Shay can, loops her arm through Fin's, and guides us over to the center of the shop. She explains several dildos and vibrators to Fin that, in fairness, look more like art pieces than sex toys. He asks questions, eyes several items seriously, and then finally settles on a vibrator.

I watch, surprised by how open Fin continues to be. Of course, it doesn't hurt that he never stops glancing my way and giving me that crooked smile that sends my heart into flight. Damn him.

On our way out of the store, there's a gorgeous display of hand-painted jewelry, and I stop to check it out. The piece that catches my eyes is a deep blue leather cuff covered in an ornately detailed peacock's feather.

"I thought ye dinna like to be restrained?"

"These are jewelry. Completely different." The price tag is no small thing, so I admire but keep walking. "We should get home. We have a vibrator to try out tonight. You're the one who'll be restrained anyway."

That gets his attention. "Wait, this is for me?" He holds up the neatly wrapped, lacy bag containing his purchase.

I grin. "Of course. Who else would it be for?"

He makes a show of turning around to go back in.

"Where are you going?" I ask, laughing and grabbing his arm.
"I'm exchanging it for a smaller one."

Chapter 13

Behind the Barn Door

It's been two days, and I miss him. Terribly. I'm pathetic, I know. But Fin's like no one I've ever been around: easy to smile, honest, and without guile. It doesn't hurt that he's completely infatuated with all things Lux Trace, I admit. Unlike previous partners, he has his own interests and passions, and he shares them openly and with gusto. I actually *look forward* to hearing his thoughts, and while it's only been a couple of weeks, I find myself thinking of excuses to text him, call him, or even better, see him in person.

Which is why I'm driving down a dusty back road right now, praying I don't ruin my rented car's paint job with the flying gravel. I'm somewhere outside the city, heading north. The mountain ranges loom, stark and foreboding. Or at least, I've always seen them that way, with their rocky hides and foggy silhouettes. I don't know where I am. I pull over to review the map, then recheck the address he gave me for the horse farm he works at. And because I'm a total teenaged girl, I reread our texts.

I miss your cock.

You have no idea how much I miss that pale skin and hot mouth of yours.

Even now, my skin is no doubt pink with delight.

Hm... You should tell me more about that.

You mean the part about how I feel like a god when I have my cock inside you? Or the part where I want to pleasure you with my mouth, my tongue buried between your thighs?

I sigh. That was all from yesterday. Or was it two mornings ago, after the night we initiated the new vibrator? I squeeze my legs together at the instant arousal from my memory of the evening. Regardless, I had clients the last two nights, and we've been relying on sexy messaging to get us through. So this morning, he sent me this.

I cannot go another day without at least tasting you, smelling you, feeling your skin against me.

We should do something about that. :)

I'm working. But you are welcome to visit.

I felt weird about that, so I'd replied:

It's okay. I can see you later.

I've seen you at work. Turnabout is fair play, right?

Given that this is one of the few Saturdays I've had off in my career as a Dom, it isn't like I had other pressing things to do. Besides… my hands were shaking, and my stomach fluttered up near my throat at the idea of seeing him again. We won't even talk about the state of my underwear. Dammit. How the fuck did this happen so fast? How did I go from mildly interested to seriously hung up?

My inner diva whined, but my sex drive hummed happily. We know who's going to win this argument, right?

So here I am, driving out to God's country on the outskirts of bumfuck, pulling up to a farm that is nothing like what I've imagined. I guess I always pictured farms and cows together. This farm has acres as far as the eye can see, with fenced off sections, some with horses grazing and others bare of life. The barns run in long lines that seem never-ending from the entrance. A manor house sits at the far end, surrounded by signs of children and the detritus of life lived quietly.

I study the trucks and cars parked across from the barns, but I have no idea what Fin drives or where to find him. What the fuck am I doing?

I park, my economy rental the odd man out amid the BMWs, Escalades, and Chevy trucks. I was smart enough to wear flat boots (original Doc Martens, for the win), but I went a little crazy on the outfit, complete with ponytails and cherry lip balm. And I probably should have thought more about the environment before I did so I realize as I shade my eyes from the blaring sun. It's a rare Northeast fall day, where the temperatures are almost seventy degrees, as though summer is having one last temper tantrum before giving in. I survey the grounds for a glimpse of Fin. No luck, so I reach for my phone, turning so I can see the screen in the bright noon light. Mid-texting, I feel arms around my waist.

"Hello there," Fin whispers in my ear, his lips brushing the sensitive spot along the bottom of my hair line.

I turn to find his mouth seeking mine, and for the moment, there is nothing more right than being in his arms, his lips hungry against my own. His hands seek purchase lower and discover my short skirt hides little else underneath.

"What's this? Did ye forget yer knickers, lass?" he teases as he trails kisses over my jaw and neck.

My fingers twine in his hair, the heat of the sun nothing compared to the inferno blazing through me. "Last I checked, Scottish men wear nothing beneath their kilts, so I figured it would be disrespectful to go against tradition."

His mouth silences me, and I nip the fullness of his bottom lip and am rewarded with a growl.

"Jesus, woman, ye're killing me."

"That's my job." I smile up at him.

With a finger, he traces my cheek, the tip falling into my very prominent dimple before reaching my chin. "Ye're good at it. But I probably shouldn't ravish ye here. Can I show ye around?"

"Sure. I'm curious."

He eyes my clothing, his gaze wandering over my white, button-down shirt atop my pleated, red plaid micro-skirt, finished with black thigh-highs and garters. "Ye might make a bit of a stir in the barn." He smiles, his light eyes crinkling at the corners. "Aye, ye'll definitely make today...interesting."

Taking my hand, he walks beside me, pointing out the paddocks, the main barn, and the auxiliary barns, along with several other sheds and such. He points out his own apartment, located over one of two old garages, and while it isn't fancy, it looks well-kept. His accent, always pronounced, becomes even more so as he describes what they do, his passion for it ebullient. Eripio Farm is, simply, a rehabilitation farm. Horses who have either had trauma or have behavioral issues—or both—come here for treatment. John Littes, Fin's mentor, is world-renown for his work with troubled horses and his unique methods of building relationships with them.

Fin guides me inside, introducing me to a few farmhands that nod politely.

"I was about to work with Nellie, if ye want to watch."

"Please. That would be great." The smell of the animals, manure, and hay combined with the indulgent odor of leather, is surprisingly pleasant. Relaxing, even. And I find myself drawn to the velvet noses that peek out as I wander while I wait for him to get Nellie out of her stall.

"Here, give them this." A boy, around age eight, hands me a couple of greenish brown cubes. They barely fit in my palms, but I examine them.

"What are they?"

"Alfalfa cubes. They love 'em. They're treats," he explains, his expression suggesting he finds me a bit dumb.

I juggle the cubes into one hand, then hold out the other. "I'm Lux."

"That's a weird name." He eyes me curiously, then shakes with a grubby paw. "Will."

"Good to meet you, Will."

"Willie-boy, aren't ye supposed to be in the house? I heard yer mum calling for ye, didn't I?"

The boy glances up as Fin approaches with a huge tan horse tethered beside him. "Yessir." And Will jettisons off.

"Little bugger. He likes to get me in trouble as he tries to hang out with me whenever I'm working." Fin smiles. "But he's a good kid."

"Seems like it," I agree, then hold up the cube. "What do I do with these?"

The horse's ears immediately prick forward, and she raises her nose.

"Ye'll have Nellie's undying affection if ye offer her one. Here." He takes my hand, places one in my palm, and directs my hand to Nellie's nose. With surprising delicacy, her big lips pluck it from my fingers.

I laugh. "She's quite the lady."

"Aye, she is. When she wants to be, isn't that right, girl?" He scratches her ears, and I offer her another cube. "Ye've not been around horses much then?"

I shake my head. "Nope. I petted one at a fair one time, I think. Come to think of it, I might have even ridden it. But this is probably the first time in my life I've been on any kind of farm."

"T'is a crime. Come. Let me show ye what Nellie here can do."

We walk to a round pen made of metal fences set in a circle, with one large gate that's open. He leads Nellie inside, closing the gate behind them while I stand on the outside.

"What is she?" I ask, unsure if that's the right way to ask about her pedigree. "I've never seen a horse that looks quite like her."

He offers me one of his cockeyed smiles. "This girl's a quarter horse, which is common enough. If ye're asking about her coloring, she's a buckskin."

I don't know what any of that means, but I nod as though it makes sense. He removes the lead and halter from her head, giving me the terms as he moves around the horse. He attends to her slowly, guiding his hands over her barrel and flank, and when he stops at certain spots, her ears flatten against her head, her back feet shifting ominously.

"What happened to her?"

He's unflustered by her mannerisms. He pulls a funny looking grooming instrument out of one pocket and rubs it over her hide. "She was with someone who should never be around animals. Used to beat the tar out of her and shove sharp fingernails into her when she didn't obey. It took years for someone to report the cruel woman. So now Nellie's here, and we'll retrain her so she can be adopted through the rescue program."

"That's amazing."

He has an ease around her, despite her wariness, and after ten minutes or so, Nellie visibly relaxes. Eventually, he backs up, clucks to her, and tells her in a soft voice, "Walk, Nellie."

He steps forward a bit, angling his body, and sure enough, Nellie starts to move. I jump when she bucks, kicking her legs out towards him, but he dodges her easily and follows her as she begins to circle him at a jagged speed around the pen. He tells her to walk again, but she ignores him, ears pinned back and nose flared, her mouth salivating wildly as she gallops the perimeter as though demons are chasing her. And I realize, they very well may be.

I wonder that he's safe, but he's completely unaffected by her. "Easy, girl," he coos, his "girl" coming out as "gehl," and seems soothing enough to me. And after her initial bouts of fear, Nellie calms to a nervous trot. After a few more minutes, his soft syllables—too quiet for me to understand—ease her temper, and she finally slows to a walk.

Eventually, she turns and walks up to him, facing him with her head cautiously dropped.

"Wow, you *are* a horse whisperer. What did you say to her?"

He lifts his hand, scratching her neck with slow strokes. "Oh, that? Nothing, actually. I just whispered an old Gaelic lullaby my gran used to sing. There's nothing I can say that will shake her terrors, Lux. Just patience, and letting her know that I'm here, ye ken? And when she comes into the ring like this," he moves around her now, sliding his hands over her, "it means she's ready to work."

I admire the thick ropes of muscle that harden his forearms as he passes those strong arms over Nellie's back and side. She stands still, her ears twitching, but by far the most relaxed she's been. When he moves into the working portion of her exercise, they communicate with nothing but bodies and words, his shifting and stepping with spoken commands, and Nellie speeding up and slowing down along the edge of the ring. At times he has to stand still and ignore her rebellion to get her to listen to him, but the session proceeds with minimal drama. It's fascinating to see this strange, intimate connection.

When she's fully lathered in sweat—as is he—he allows her to come into the center with him again, and he redresses her in her halter and lead.

'That was incredible," I say, and I mean it. "How do you do it? How did you get her from bucking bronco to obedient?"

He grins, pleasure over my compliment lighting his face beneath the grime from the ring. "Ye know, it's not about obedience. Not really. It's more about creating a relationship. A partnership, if ye will. She outweighs me by more than fifty stone or so. I'm not going to win against her in a fight, ye ken." He nods to the big horse. "And she would like to fight me, no doubt to work off some of the cruelty of her past. When she submits, like ye saw her do, it's then that she acknowledges our equality, ye see. We come into that moment together, nurturing the relationship."

What he says makes sense, but there's a strange keening inside me at his words. I stay quiet and walk back to the barn with him.

"Would ye like to get some lunch? There's a barbecue stand down the road a few kilometers." He looks down at his filthy jeans and t-shirt. "I'll get cleaned up, and we'll go if ye want."

"Sure. Sounds good."

I walk the barns while I wait, fascinated by the alternate world that exists so far outside of the bright lights and showy world of the city. I'm also a bit embarrassed by how I'm dressed, so I avoid treading anywhere that I hear voices. I end up in an old office, where faded show ribbons hang from the walls, collecting dust, and black and white pictures mingle with color images. All of them have horses and riders, and they represent something I've never experienced before—competition. Playing odds you could lose. And it occurs to me that perhaps that is what is bothering me lately. My life, despite the daring that others perceive it has, is safe. I am always in control of my interactions and sexual escapades. I choose, and while I'm not sure I always make the right decisions, there is no risk involved, either. Of course, with Kinked, all that is changing.

Does Fin bring with him the same danger of losing control and taking chances? While the more I'm around him, the deeper I fall for him…it also dredges up darkness that I haven't contended with in some time.

I'm lost in thought when I hear Fin's voice calling my name. He finds me leaning against the desk, reading the accolades on the wall.

"Ye wondered into no man's land, eh?"

"Hm?"

"This barn needs its roof replaced, and it's not been used for some time. It's sturdy enough, but given that we board animals for people, they don't want to risk a lawsuit in case something would happen."

The scent of soap and wintergreen tickles my nose, and when Fin leans down to kiss me, I respond with a passion borne from my tempestuous thoughts. His hands seek my thighs, lifting me so my legs grasp his waist. His jeans press against my bare flesh, and I suck in a breath as his hands spread my ass and hold me even tighter against him.

"I want to be inside ye, Lux," he says against my mouth.

"Can the door be locked?"

"Aye, but I have a bigger problem."

I chuckle. "I can feel that."

He rests his forehead against mine. "Aye, well, that's not all. I dinna have any protection on me. I can run back to my apartment—"

I press my lips to his. "I'm tested and clean."

"I am as well, but I dinna want you to think—"

"Fuck me," I say and shove my tongue in his mouth, eliminating any further argument.

Our breaths collide as our passions rise, and I rub against the harsh texture of his jeans, enjoying his trapped erection.

"I must have ye on my cock." He sets me on my feet so he can lock the door, then he unfastens his belt and jeans. He pulls me to him again, mouth hot on my neck and collarbone. His naked cock caught between us, I shift my stomach against it, earning a groan from him. I unbutton my shirt, slipping out of it as he reaches for my bra. I'm left only in my boots and plaid skirt. The dim room is cool, but I don't feel it as I bend down to take him in my mouth. He grips my arms, though, lifting me to my feet and turning me so my back presses against his chest.

"I'm going to take ye hard, love, as hard as ye took me that night ye tied me down."

His hand grips my breast, squeezing so hard I nearly cry out, but the pain fuels my passion, and when he bends me over the desk, I want to object, but the feel of his hand on my hip, his cock throbbing against me, is too much, and all I want is Fin. Inside me. Now.

He fills me with one thrust, and I feel as though I'm being torn in two. His thick cock spreads me so wide, I can barely gasp. When he pulls out, I suck air, but then he surges back into me, one hand holding me still, the other pinching my nipple with a vise-like grip. And I love it. Even as he fucks me hard and I'm nearly senseless with desire, I realize that I've never been quite like this—so out of control, and so desperate for someone else to give me what I need. He slaps my ass, first lightly, then harder, and the snap of pain sends my orgasm soaring. I want to scream as I explode inside, but he covers my mouth, slipping a finger between my lips as I fight to avoid making noise.

He leans over me, my body pinioned on his cock, his arms holding me against his body. "Did I hurt ye? Are ye okay?"

I nod. "Don't stop," I whisper hoarsely.

So he doesn't. Pressing me to the desk, he reaches even deeper inside me, his cock seeming to grow larger with each thrust, and as he fucks me, he spares no mercy. Another climax threatens me, even as my legs grow weak, and when I can take no more intensity, it ruptures through me anyway, decimating any defenses I might have built, and lands with a ferocity that leaves me nearly unconscious in its wake.

Chapter 14
Switch

"Oh my God. This is probably the best barbecue I've ever had." Juice drips down my hands from the sandwich, and I ignore it in favor of the bliss assaulting my taste buds. "I may never eat anything else."

We're at, quite literally, a "stand" that sits on the side of the road. With the exception of a few small plastic tables and chairs, the food is meant to be taken to go.

I'm also delighted to discover that Fin drives an old truck, one he borrows from the farm. While I've never had any cowboy fantasies, there is something incredibly sexy about a guy in a roughed-up pickup. So we drop the tailgate, spread an old, horsey blanket we found behind the seats, and nosh homemade pulled-pork sandwiches and fresh-cut french fries.

Fin smiles. "I've been quite fond of this place since I discovered it, but then, I dinna know much about barbecue to begin with. Glad you like it." He takes a bite of his own sandwich, which requires a certain amount of strategy so the soft bun doesn't fall apart around the meat. We sit in companionable silence until we're finished, then we start on the fries.

"Any more word from yer investors?"

"It's happening. I just got the call to set up a time with their liaison to sign the papers. I guess they have some kind of rule from the CEO that all deals are signed in person with one of their people. They're coming to me, so I can't complain." I swipe a fry through ketchup.

"Are ye excited?"

I realize that I'm frowning, so I grin. "Yes. I am. But a bit nervous. This is a huge change for me. And while I love what I do…this could get in the way of it."

"Being a Dominatrix, ye mean?"

I nod, munching. It occurs to me that I have no idea how he feels about my career. "Does it bother you? What I do for a living?"

He leans back against the truck, moving his leg so he's still touching me. "No. Why should it?"

I rake my gaze over him, enjoying the way his chest fills out his t-shirt. "Well, it's something that could bother a partner. I'm intimate with the fantasies of my clients, and while I don't sleep with them," *anymore,* I say to myself, "it's still pretty sexual at its core." I meet his squinting eyes. "That doesn't bother you even a little?"

He ponders for a moment, his lips pressed together. "I *wasna* bothered…" He flashes me a smile, his dimple in full effect. "I'd be a bit more concerned if ye were sleeping with a bunch of other people, I suppose. But I'm not particularly jealous of the person ye're beating with yer wee whips." He snorts and mocks a shiver. "Rather them than me."

I can't help but chuckle. "Point taken."

Despite the warm day, when he leans forward to run a hand over my arm, I get goosebumps at the contact. "I want ye to be happy, Lux. I'm not looking for a relationship with multiple people, mind ye. That's not who I am. I care about ye, and what ye do is part of what makes ye who ye are. After all, I thought ye had sex with clients when I asked ye out." He pauses for a moment, an embarrassed smile playing at the corners of his mouth. He chuckles softly when I give him a cocked eyebrow. "Aye, well, I dinna say I was particularly brilliant about the way I did it. But I shouldna have asked ye out if I dinna accept what ye did."

"Wow." I whistle in admiration. "Where did you get so open-minded?"

He ponders for a moment, then says with a furrowed brow. "I dinna know, honestly. My parents are very traditional in their beliefs, but they're progressive enough. I was raised with a mind of my own, if ye will."

"Are your siblings like you?" I know he's from a relatively large family—compared to my own, anyway—but while he's mentioned them a few times, we haven't gotten around to the big "family tree" exchange, particularly because I avoid it so deftly.

"Aye, more or less." He collects our trash, then rejoins me on the tailgate. "Ye're an only child?"

I fiddle with my sunglasses. "I almost forgot to ask—how are your applications with the colleges going?"

"I called yesterday, as a matter of fact. I haven't heard anything from Cornell, and since my application for next term was barely in under the deadline, I dinna ken if they'll let me start."

"So if you do, you'll start in January."

"That's my hope." He reaches for my hand, his fingers linking with mine. "Ye dinna like to talk about yer family much."

I trace the outline of our fingers with my other hand. "It's a good day. Let's not go there."

He squints against the sun but doesn't look away. "Fair enough. But I'm not going to run away if ye're related to the Sasquatch, love."

I chuckle. "Thanks, I think." The mood is broken, so we head back. Fin drops me off at my car, and for the first time in my life, I make out in a pickup. There's definitely something to be said for it.

On the way home, though, unwelcome thoughts come to roost. I'm not exactly sure what Fin and I are doing. Due to my reticence, we haven't had any "are we dating" discussions, and as a result, I feel a bit adrift. Which is ridiculous, because I'm the one who'd avoid "labeling" it anyway. But the intensity of my emotions when I'm in his space troubles me. I'm not one apt to fall in love, and this feels dangerously close to it. The cons of getting involved with him mount in my head, and I feel gloomier with each mile.

One: He's not here permanently. If he doesn't get into college, he'll have to go home. Two: He's just starting college and considering his career. While there may only be five—five!—years difference between us, where we are at in life is vastly different. 3: …

I rack my brain to think of another con. Being shockingly good-looking and ridiculously nice and open-minded aren't flaws. And when I think of him inside me earlier in the barn…I've had a lot of fun sex over the years—it comes with the territory. But there's a passion to sex with Fin that I haven't experienced in a long time. Perhaps ever. He submits easily, but he likes taking over as well. I don't know how I feel about that. I've spent a long time in the driver's seat in most of my romantic and sexual relationships. I don't know if I'm cut out for a relationship where I'm not the one in control 100% of the time.

And *that* thought makes me really uncomfortable. What kind of partner am I if I can't share the reins? Who am I if I do?

The shower turns on, and I gather my equipment, returning each piece—crop, rubber whip, paddle—to its place. I pack up my restraints and gag, all of which will be washed when I get home. Then I perch on the edge of the bed, still in my corset and thigh-high boots, though I've pulled my trench coat over my ensemble.

When Charles walks back into the bedroom of the hotel suite, he looks refreshed, lighter in step, and he smiles widely. "Once again, Mistress Hathaway, I can't thank you enough."

Charles's desire for conversation after his sessions continues, and I've come to genuinely like him. He's intelligent, and though I don't know much about him, he seems polite and well-read. I can't quite guess what he does for a living, but I've no doubt it's something impressive. It must be, given the cost of this room and my services.

"My pleasure as always," I say on rote, though I truly do mean it. I'm not completely present in the moment, and I can't quite figure out why.

He looks at me. "You seem a bit distracted. Not that I didn't enjoy myself, of course," he's quick to add. "But I did notice a bit of shadow behind your eyes."

His intuitive comment shakes my facade. "I apologize. I didn't mean that to affect your—"

"No, no, it didn't. But I've been seeing you twice a week for…oh, about a month or so now? And today, you seem…not quite yourself. May I be so bold as to ask if I can be of any help? Perhaps just to talk about whatever is bothering you?"

I take a deep breath. I do not get personal with my clients. Often they tell me dark secrets because I give them a safe place in which to do so, but I do not share my issues in exchange. I hold myself to these professional standards. But in this moment, I want to ask him something so badly that I can't stop the words when they spring to my lips. "I've met someone. And I don't…" I trail off, desperately wishing I could take the words back. What am I doing? My mouth, though, seems to have a mind of its own. "How did you know you were submissive?"

The question surprises him—and me—and he takes a seat on the edge of the settee across from the bed. "That's a good question. I think I've always known. I knew when I was a child, and I would imagine my teachers putting me in a corner, tying me down, spanking me; unfortunately, by then, spanking in schools had been forbidden." His eyes glint in humor. "But I think I've always been this way. How about you? How did you know you were dominant?"

I ponder his query. "When I started having hormones, probably. I knew I liked to be on top, to have that say in my own pleasure."

"Have you ever tried bottoming? Or being submissive at all?"

I think uncomfortably of last week, at the barn. While I wasn't submissive, per se, the power had definitely shifted between Fin and me, and rather than being turned off by it, I felt unbelievably turned on. I'd wanted him to force me to his will. When he spanked me, I'd exploded with desire. What did that make me? That certainly wasn't the behavior of a Dominant. "No, I haven't," I say, not sure that it's still the truth, but not having another answer I'm willing to give. "It's never appealed to me."

Charles's full lips turn up, his dark eyes not missing a thing. "You might be surprised. Not meaning any disrespect, Mistress, but there is something delightful about experiencing both sides. I assure you, being out of control, letting someone else carry that burden for a while, and simply experiencing pleasure that is all your own...there's nothing like it."

I narrow my eyes at him. "Are you saying you're a switch, Charles?"

He chuckles. "No, I'm most certainly not. But I am saying that if you've never at least tried both sides, how can you know if you don't like it? And while switches may not be common, they aren't exactly rare, either." He stands then, as I do.

I gather my bag and tie my coat around me. He walks me to the door and takes my hands. "You won't be less of a Dom if you decide to play on the sub-side, Mistress. Quite the opposite. Perhaps only one who has enjoyed the pleasure of both can truly understand the fullness of their preferences."

I don't want to know how he's reading my fears and doubts, so I paste a smile on my face. "Interesting observations, Charles."

He squeezes my fingers gently and bows his head. "Thank you for my punishment, Mistress Hathaway. I will endeavor to be less naughty for you."

When I'm in the Town Car, headed to Brooklyn, his words turn over in my mind. Am I less of a Dom because I've never submitted before? Is there something else driving me to always be in control? These questions make me uncomfortable. They make me question everything that I am, and none of it gives me any peace. As the car whisks me home, I put on earbuds, the Ramones blaring in my ears, visions of Nellie's fear edging the perimeter of my thoughts.

Chapter 15
Reflection

Halloween is always fun in the BDSM world. Given that there are whole fetishes dedicated to dressing up as just about anything—squirrels, horses, monsters—having an excuse to publicly take the show on the road ensures that Paddled is packed the whole week. Usually, I make an event of it, choosing sexy costumes for a couple different evenings, and head to the club to embrace the crazed fun of the week.

This year, I don't. Whether it's related to the confusing thoughts I've been struggling with or perhaps just a phase, I hide out at home.

Elementary has gotten even busier, so Noah's barely home, and when he is, he's glued to his computer. We haven't gone out for a good time in ages, and I haven't the heart to interrupt him most days, but for once, I notice the strain in his posture, so I make a bit of noise in the kitchen to avoid startling him.

"Did you eat dinner yet?"

"Hm?" He looks up at me, a bit dazed.

"Dinner. The meal that often comes after lunch and before your midnight snack. Did you have it yet?"

He leans back in his chair, his handsome face bracketed with lines of stress. "I don't think I had breakfast, so no, I'm pretty sure I haven't had dinner yet."

"You want to order in?"

He considers, then shakes his head. "Let's go out. We haven't done that in a long time."

"Should we call Ella? See if she can put Ian on nanny patrol?"

"No point. Mia's been running a low-grade fever, and it's probably nothing. But Ella won't leave her until she's—"

"Eighteen, I know." I smile.

He nods. "Probably. But let's you and I go. We'll make a night of it."

Thirty minutes later, we're on the street, hoofing it towards our favorite bar that's not too far from the house. We order drinks and dinners, then settle back into the thick wooden chairs and size each other up.

"You're in love."

His words surprise me so much, I'm stunned into silence. I stare down at my napkin and silverware, running my fingertip over the tines of my fork, again and again.

"And you haven't told him yet, have you?"

"What are you, the love psychic?" Why can't I just have a nice dinner without my personal life coming up to slap me in the face? Oh, right, because Noah's one half of my duo of best friends, and they are also possibly empaths.

"I don't know about psychic, but I recognize the signs. Plus, you have that strange glow women get when they're in love."

"I don't have a glow," I snap, but it loses heat when I can't help chuckling.

"Yes, you do." He eyes me closely. "And it looks good on you."

I roll my eyes. "How about you? Made a love connection with online dating yet?"

Now it's his turn to examine the utensils. "Love would be a strong word."

I drop the napkin I've been unfolding onto my lap. "What? You met someone?"

He wags his head noncommittally. "I might have found a few women intriguing."

"A few? As in, more fuck 'em and dump 'em dates? Or actual first dates with possibilities for seconds?"

With a small smile, he changes the subject. "So is the ink dry on the official partnership with Divine, Inc.?"

"God. What a mess. Nance, the woman I was supposed to meet with to do the deed, got injured while skiing in Colorado, so the meeting was postponed until next week. Of course, they won't pay for anything until the paperwork is completed." I trail off, wishing we'd ordered in and watched *The Matrix* trilogy.

"Lulu, it's all going to work out. Divine is in this. It's all over but the dancing." He smiles encouragingly.

"I know. Nance assured me the delay is no big deal. The CEO is really funny about their investment agreements being made in person, as she feels it builds relationships within their company and network. And I totally agree. But still. The waiting is making me jumpy." I shift the subject, and we spend the rest of night talking about movies and friends.

In bed that night, I can't sleep. In my core, I know that I need to do something new and different; Kinked is that something. Reviewing the bids and ideas of the contractors not only excites me, but it's the first time I've felt alive in a long time.

I love being a Dominatrix. At least, I used to love it. And I still do…some days. But I want something that uses more of my skills as a business woman, rather than just my skills in the bedroom. Not to mention, I'm not sure if this is the best place for me right now, given my broken rules and guilt. I haven't slept with anyone but Fin since we've been together. Hell, I haven't *wanted* to sleep with anyone else.

There's also the part where it's hard to have a relationship with someone when you're in a sensual trade. Stripper, escort, Dominatrix, etc.…we all have complications that make even the most open-minded lover question on occasion. Despite Fin's insistence that he's fine with it, I don't know if I am. I know—weird, right? I should be totally cool with everything. But I'm not.

I punch my pillow, then shove it back into position, but my bed is lonely. Fin traveled to another farm today for a consultation, so I won't see him until tomorrow night. And that I'm even missing him this much…it feels so out of character. Yet just thinking about his warm skin and luscious mouth has my stomach doing flip-flops of excitement. More than that, I wish he was beside me, even just to sleep.

It's going to be a long night.

Chapter 16

The Highlander

 I apply a last thick coat of mascara, then step back to examine my art. Fin and I have not one, but two Halloween parties for tonight, and given that they will be as different as night and day, I wasn't sure what costume to wear. So I went for a combination "goth faery." A blood red corset and tulle skirt, under a layer of black mesh, knee boots with stiletto heels, barely-there silver and black wings that spread out behind my shoulders, and my hair in pigtails with glitter and silver spray-on hair color. I went heavy on the eye makeup, but with a light pink lip, and some glitter and shimmer on my skin. I'm pleased with the overall result as I angle my body before the mirror.

 I've no idea what Fin decided to do for a costume, though I admit to being curious. Noah already left for the party at his sister's, so I answer the door when the doorbell sounds.

 A tall, well-built Scotsman with a handsome face is never hard on the eyes. That same Scotsman in a traditional kilt with all the trimmings? Glorious.

 "At yer service, m'lady," Fin greets me with a small, courtly bow before handing me a single red rose.

 My smile spreads so wide my cheeks ache, and I find myself biting my lip. "Wow. You look phenomenal. Is this legit? Like a real kilt?"

 "Ye slay me, m'lady," he mocks, holding his hands over his heart as though I've wounded him. "Ye'd expect any less of a descendent of the Scottish highlanders?"

I laugh but welcome his warm mouth to mine as he cautiously slides his hands around my cinched waist, neatly avoiding the ties of the wings.

"When ye told me about the parties, I had my mum send over my da's tartan. It's what he married in, ye see."

"It's stunning."

"Aye, well, ye look a fair angel yerself. And what are ye, winged creature?"

I turn and curtsy. "A lone goth faery, at your service."

He smiles appreciatively, wiggling his eyebrows. "Did ye remember your knickers this time, love? Or might I have the pleasure of taking advantage of yer wee skirt?"

With a chuckle, I wag a finger at him. "You'll have to hold off on your naughtiness until later tonight," I say as I flash him my boy-short-covered backside, "as I don't want to scar my godchild with my lack of propriety."

He takes my hand and walks me to his car. "I rather like yer lack of propriety. That's one of my favorite things about ye." He pulls me in for another kiss, his fingers grazing the curve of my jaw as he looks down at me afterwards. "One of many."

Ella and Ian live on Long Island, so we opted to drive. I whistle when we reach the car. "Wow, again. Are you going to get picked up for grand theft auto before the night's over?"

He looks down at the cobalt blue 5-series BMW, then back at me. "Aye, well, Stephen said I couldna be picking ye up in the truck, so he lent me this for…well, I have the distinct feeling he wants me to keep it for a bit, as he seemed a bit shocked that ye'd been riding around in such a filthy beast."

I snort but am not surprised. "Given that Stephen collects cars like some people collect shot glasses, I doubt he'll miss it." The car is stunning, and while I prefer a more vintage look, there's no denying the comfort of its supple leather and heated seats.

"How did you meet Stephen? I keep meaning to ask."

Fin settles into the driver's seat. "Och, that's a story. Ye'll remember that I came to the States in the beginning of the summer? I wasna here more than a month when one of the barn hands suggested we go out. I think she might have had a bit of a crush on me."

"Imagine that," I comment dryly.

He ignores me and continues. "So I met her at a small bar, and before we were an hour in, she was wasted. I dinna know what to do with her, but I couldna very well leave her there."

"Let me guess: you were at Cavalier?" Stephen's co-owner of the wildly successful Cavalier, a European-esque bar for locals.

"Aye. And Stephen was there. He thought I needed a bit of 'tending,' as he put it."

I snickered. "I bet he did. I suppose modeling for underwear and volunteering you as a third with me was included in his 'tending'?"

He glanced over at me and grinned. "Aye, well, I canna argue with the man's genius. I'd pose half-naked several times over as long as it leads me to you."

An involuntary smile spreads over my face, and I reach for his hand, squeezing it. The ride to the first party is fairly short, and Fin whistles between his teeth as we pull up to Ella and Ian's palatial estate.

"Ye dinna tell me we were visiting the wealthy side of the family. Glad Stephen lent me his BMW." He pulls into the driveway, though other, mostly high-end cars already line the long drive and have pulled onto the yard. We follow suit and head for the house.

"So these are friends of yers, yes?"

I grin. "Don't sound so nervous. I live with Noah—you've met him in passing, I think?"

He shakes his head. "No, he's never been there when I have."

I think about it. "You're right. Well, they've been really busy with Elementary," I say by way of apology. "Anyway, Ella is Noah's sister, and she and her husband Ian—he's a corporate lawyer, but he also comes from money—have the baby I showed you pictures of."

He nods but continues to stare at the house.

Inside the manse, people in costumes mill about, some talking and drinking, others eating, and the general air is festive. Carved pumpkins and antique lanterns fill corners, while twinkle lights and cheerful looking ghouls and ghosts set the scene. There's barely room to squeeze into the living area, but I can see Ian's dark head above the crowd, and where he is, I'm bound to find Ella.

There's a cool trickle of nerves down my back. Ella has yet to meet Fin, and while her approval is not critical…I want her to like him. Glancing behind me, I realize that he really *is* nervous. I take his hand, pulling him close. "They're going to love you." I look up into his dazzling blue-green eyes, and he smiles in return.

"Aye, well, there's not much I can do if they don't, I suppose." His expression softens. "As long as ye do, that's all that matters."

We haven't broached the "L" word, which, really, it's only been… six weeks? Seven? Is there some criteria for when such things should be discussed? Nonetheless, fear snakes through my gut, and I force it away. I press my lips to his briefly, then lead him to my friends.

Ella wears a stunning red dress, complete with horns and a cape. When she sees me, she nearly squeals. "Oh my God, look at you. I love it! Come here." She pulls me into an embrace, careful of the wings, but I feel her notice Fin over my shoulder. "So this is the hunk of Scottish lust behind you, eh?" she whispers in my ear.

I introduce Fin to Ella, and she nods approvingly in my direction. I roll my eyes, but inwardly, I'm pleased. When Ian finishes his conversation, he leans down to buss my cheek and greets Fin with a handshake.

"Wait—I've met you before. You were at my parents' farm, working with the new filly."

"Aye, sir, and a fine girl she was, too."

The two men start talking horses, and Ella and I share a glance that says, *men*.

"Where's my adorable godchild?"

"Come with me." Ella leads me to the library where she's closed the doors to keep people out. "All the excitement was a bit too much for my darling. But she's out like a light anyway." She sighs, reaching down inside the travel crib. Her finger follows the curve of Mia's cheek, and even in sleep, the baby turns towards it, her mouth curling in a half smile.

Babies are cute in general, but this child is especially beautiful, if I do say so myself. She's dressed as a piece of candy corn, and I snag a photo of her with my cell phone. "Argh, I was hoping I'd get to hold her."

Ella snorts lightly, careful not to wake Mia. "Trust me, you don't want to." She gestures to a small stain on her dress, unnoticeable until she points it out. "My child is adorable, but her need to mark every single damn piece of clothing is wearing thin quickly." She levels a gaze at Mia, but her annoyance quickly fades to affection.

"Sit with me," she says, gesturing to a small couch along the back wall of the room.

While the noise of the party permeates, there is a hushed stillness with a sleeping child, and it's surprisingly relaxing.

"So…spill." She narrows her light blue eyes, so similar to her brother's that it's a bit eerie at times. "Who's the new guy? And hello, can we say hot *and* Scottish?"

I shrug, feeling the heat crawling into my cheeks. "There's not much to say. We've been dating for…a month and a half? Maybe a little longer—"

"Wait, it's been that long, and I'm just now meeting him? What's with the secrecy, woman?" She's teasing, but there's a bit of hurt beneath it, I think.

"Hardly keeping him a secret. I told you about him when we went to dinner forever ago." I nudge her shoulder with mine. "Last I checked, you're swamped with motherhood, a full-time business, and a husband."

Her face drops. "I'm a horrible friend."

"No, no! That's not what I mean. It's just…you've been busy. And I get that. We haven't hung out in a long time, like we used to. And it's okay. That's what happens when you have a family."

She shakes her head. "No, Lux, it's me. Ian's pushed me to get out of the house more than just for work. We even have a nanny for the days I'm working with Noah. Between Mia running fevers, writing murder mysteries, and parties galore, I've been…" She stops herself, then seems to change her mind. "No, this is my fault. I know you've been trying to work on your own business, and I've been so consumed, I haven't even asked about it. I'm sorry."

This conversation is not turning out as I thought it would. "It's okay, really. I get it, Ells. Truly."

She hugs me, her arms strong, and she kisses the side of my head. "Love you. We need to have a standing date. Every week." She thinks for a moment. "Maybe every other week?"

I laugh. "How about, we'll pick a regular night, and we'll take turns at each other's abodes? That way, you don't always have to leave the fort untended."

She agrees, but her hand reaches for mine. "Are you feeling any better about things?"

I don't know how to answer her question. Am I feeling better? When I'm with Fin, of course. When I'm working, I'm fine. But my worries over Kinked continue to mount—even though I've finally scheduled another date to meet with Nance one week from today. These aren't topics for a party, however, so I squeeze her fingers. "I'm good." I smile and nod to punctuate the statement, and that seems to satisfy her.

Returning to the party, Ella introduces me to more names and faces than I will ever remember, but then a dark-haired, tall man steps beside her, and I have no problem recognizing him.

"Mick!" Ella reaches for the A-list actor Mick Jeffries, hugging him close, then does the same with his wife, a well-known starlet who just won an award for best supporting actress. I've met them before, so more hugs are exchanged, and we chat for a while. He's one of the many celebrities Ella and Noah have planned parties for.

I check on Fin out of the corner of my eye, but he and Ian are talking with a bunch of people, and he seems completely at ease. His kilt shows off his muscular calves, and the cream shirt ties in the front, revealing just a hint of his chiseled collarbone and chest. When he catches my eye, he smiles sweetly, but there's suggestion beneath it, and my core heats up.

Down, girl.

It's several hours later when I catch up to him. "Hey, social butterfly, we should probably get going," I whisper when I track him down near the traditional punch bowl.

"I nearly forgot. Let me just say good-bye to Ian and his wife."

We trail over to them, and with lots of hugs and kisses to send us on our way, we head for the BMW.

"Now, what might I expect at the next party?"

I take a breath. "The absolute opposite of this one."

Chapter 17

When in Rome

Stephen's house is on the Upper West Side, so by the time we finally find a spot to park—one of the many reasons I'll never own a car in NYC—it's just before midnight. I'm ready to shed this corset and tulle, but I paste a smile on my face as we traipse towards the door.

I grab Fin's hand. "Just remember—anything goes. Try not to stare, unless it seems welcome. And don't touch anyone, as you never know what that might get you into." I think for a second. "Oh, and don't agree to anything. He'll have several slaves ready to submit to a willing Master, so whatever happens, don't nod, say yes, or look interested. Unless you are, of course."

He makes a manly noise that sounds suspiciously like the infamous Scottish grunt. "Hmphmm. I think I'll let ye do the talking, just to be on the safe side." He curls his fingers beneath my chin, feathering a light kiss against my lips. "Ye're the only woman I wish to have mastering me...or submitting to me for that matter." He winks.

I smile, but inside, I'm quivering. We've discussed the whole let-me-tie-you-up-like-you-did-to-me thing several times. Not because he's pushed the issue, but because I don't know that I'll ever be ready for it. And I still don't know what to do about it. Yet there's a part of me that can't stop thinking about it.

Inside Stephen's large, one-story townhome, we're ushered into a dark, sophisticated dream. There's a hookah room, an artist's alley, and when you walk further back, you discover what really makes Stephen's parties a hit: the anything-goes event.

And I do mean anything.

I watch Fin's face, enjoying the play of reactions as we step into the dusky space that is normally a game room. Tonight, it's been cleared of all furniture, except for some plush chairs. Thick rugs line the hardwood floor, and given how many people are naked and in varied positions upon its lush fibers, that's probably a good thing. Heavy bass fills the air, pumping a haunting rhythm that seems alive against a backdrop of sexual energy. From BDSM and fetish play to outright sex, the orgy before us moves to its own beats and kink.

Fin bites the inside of his lip, probably to keep his jaw from dropping. "You dinna adequately describe the level of debauchery, love," he says softly in my ear.

"Have I offended your delicate sensibilities?" I return, teasing and sliding my leg between his, enjoying the feel of his cock stiffening against me.

"In many, many ways." His mouth captures mine in a sensual kiss, and the din of the room is forgotten for the moment.

We escape to the relative quiet of the artist's alley, where local creative minds offer some of their wares. It's set in the dining room, while the caterers work at a frantic pace in the kitchen. Stephen wanders by, his blond hair a beacon in the dim mood lighting.

He spots us immediately. "My doves, you made it." He wears a fashionable pair of jeans and a silk shirt, complete with leather slippers, which is so Stephen.

Stephen kisses my cheek, hugs Fin with exuberance, and then stands back. "Love the vibe you've got there, Lux. And damn, boy, you do clean up." While costumes were optional for the party, given the reasons why most people attend, they're generally not convenient. It's likely we're the only ones dressed up for the holiday.

Believe it or not, Stephen was—and still is, when a regular calls him up—a heterosexual escort, though he's not straight or gay. He describes himself as pansexual, and for as long as I've known him—since high school—that's as good a descriptor as any. When hired for a job, he's as alpha male as they come, but left to his own devices, he tends towards a more boisterous, slightly effeminate flare.

"Drinks? Food? We're just getting started."

Fin clears his throat. "Aye, well, it looks like the backroom's been going for a while."

Stephen chuckles but waves a hand. "Not even. Well, I did say a few could get started early, but trust me, this is nothing. Give it another hour. I'll have people fucking on the roof."

Given that his home is a townhouse, I rather hope that isn't the case, but I've been to Stephen's parties before. They almost always have a sexual component, and they fill up fast. I wonder if he's paid off his neighbors not to complain, because I've no idea how he gets away with this otherwise.

"How's the wheels, Fin? Enjoying the feel of luxury?"

Fin reddens a touch. "Aye, it does the job."

Stephen heaves a sigh and leans down towards me. "You can take the boy outta the country…"

I shake my head. "You think everyone should drive ridiculously expensive cars."

"And the problem with that?"

I'm saved from answering when Stephen is called away by the caterers. "Have fun, my sweets! Do *everything* I would do." With an air kiss, he heads for the kitchen.

"So…what do we do, exactly? This doesn't seem the kind of place where you 'mingle.'" Fin slips an arm around my waist.

I kiss him. "Well, we could watch. Or we could have some fun ourselves." I gauge his expression, not wanting to push him too far.

He scratches the back of his neck, giving himself away. "How about, I'll trust ye and let ye decide what we do?"

"God, you are such a man. But I love you anyway." The minute the words are out of my mouth, I'd do anything to take them back. I'm not even sure I mean them. I said them, so therefore, on some level, I must mean them, right? Shit. I'm not supposed to say *it* first. Or at least, not without some very solid intuition that it'll be returned. But I said the big "L" word. There's no going back on it now.

If he sees the fear in my eyes, I don't know. He definitely heard what I said, as when I dare to meet his gaze again, there's a softness there to which I'm not sure how to respond.

With the loud music and commotion around us, it's unlikely that I'll hear him when he leans down. But he enunciates very carefully so I don't miss a syllable.

"I love ye as well."

I know my way around, but Stephen is wise enough to lock all of the off-limits spaces. Given how full the game room is, we return to the hookah/living room. It's already been taken over by a few couples and threesomes who are getting their sexy on. I spy an overstuffed chair with an ottoman in the far corner, and we make our way to it.

"We can watch, or we can play. Or do both." I turn, laying my hands against his chest. Our exchange in the kitchen has my stomach thrumming with warmth as though I just downed a brandy, and when he reaches for my arms, he encounters goosebumps.

"You're freezing," he whispers, drawing me closer, but the wings impede the movement. With a few deft pulls, I untie them and let them slide to the floor. Then I step into the warm arms waiting for me, and for a moment, lay my head against his heart, listening to his solid rhythm.

When I look up, his eyes are molten with need, but there's a deeper emotion there that I can't deny, but I don't know how to respond to, either. So instead, I get lost in his mouth, the feel of his skin, the way his hands find every sensitive bit of exposed flesh…

"I opt for both, then." His deep voice tickles my ear, and when I look at him, there's a challenge in his gaze. I've never backed down from anything, so I simply nod. He sits in the chair, and with gentle hands, positions me between his legs, then evaluates my costume. "How does this come off?"

And this is where I didn't plan very well. Because if I take my costume off, it's going to be tricky to get back into it. Given that I have a kilted Scotsman looking at me as though I'm his next meal, I bite my lip and turn so he can access the hooks and eyes of the corset.

It takes some time, but he finally releases the last hook, and the corset sags around me, held up only by my arms. While I've never been particularly shy about my body and this isn't the first time I've been in this situation, there's a bit of hesitation before I stand naked in front of an audience. A relatively oblivious audience, but given that four more people just took up the far corner…

I slide the corset down my body, relinquishing it to the floor. I wear only the boy-shorts and skirt now; his strong fingers untie the skirt, and then he slides both down my legs. I step out of them, left in my knee-boots.

He pulls me down to his lap as he relaxes into the seat.

"Spread your legs, love."

The heat of his breath on my neck leaves me shaking. I've never responded to orders before, never been with anyone who would even consider it, but suddenly I want nothing more than to do exactly what he says, and the conflict rages inside me, even as I drape my legs over his. His one hand covers my breast as he tips my head back so he has access to my mouth. Scorching kisses leave me wet, and I dissolve in a haze of desire.

He spreads his legs, opening me up even further and putting me on display to the room. While he lightly pinches my nipple, his palm skims my stomach, stopping just north of where I want his fingers.

"Tell me something, Lux." He presses his lips to my jaw, his teeth grazing my skin. "Tell me what you want."

I swallow, unable to form the words.

"Ask me."

The sensual slapping of skin on skin, groans of pleasure, and the dim light should lower my inhibitions, but at this moment, I feel wildly exposed as erotic images I've never given voice to play across my mind, and my senses take in the sexuality of the background.

"What do you want?"

With another hard swallow, I whisper against his mouth, "Touch me."

He stills beneath me, waiting.

"Please."

His lips descend on mine with ferocity as his fingers slide over me, teasing the edge of my sex. I buck against him, desperate for friction. His mouth silences any words, quelling my rebellion.

"I will have ye, love. In my time, damn ye." He lifts one of his legs, propping his foot on the ottoman before us. Now I'm not only spread wider, but I don't have two feet on the ground, ensuring he has even more control over me.

His fingertips slip into me, but just a fraction. I nip his lip in response, earning me a soft chuckle.

"Ye're a stubborn thing, eh?" He gives me no relief, circling my tender clit.

I have no choice but to relax against him and enjoy the sensation of my captured breast and his hard cock pressed against my ass.

"I'm going to fuck you, Lux, but first, you're going to beg me to let you come." There's play in his words, but the demand is still there.

"I will never beg," I return, a slight smile on my lips as he twists my nipple with a little more pressure. I gasp, loving the intensity that borders discomfort.

He dips his fingertips inside me again. "Aye, love, ye will." He continues his sensual exploration, pressing me open, barely touching the underside of my clit before removing his fingers altogether and focusing his attention on my breasts and mouth.

I drop my head back against him when I can barely take any more, and I catch the eye of another woman directly across from us. Her lover is taking her from behind as her wrists are bound before her, and she watches Fin and I with evident enjoyment.

There's something incredibly arousing about being watched, and the tension inside me heightens. Fin finally drives his fingers into me, allowing me to grind against his palm. Even as my orgasm builds, I know he's testing me, and sure enough, as soon as I'm about to tip over the edge, he withdraws his hand.

The woman opposite me smiles knowingly when our gazes meet. Her emboldened stare invites mine, so I maintain the eye contact as Fin continues to tease me mercilessly. In retaliation, I pull at his kilt, tugging it from beneath me, so his bare cock rests between my ass cheeks.

"Now who will beg?" I say, tightening my thighs so I weigh heavily against his length, trapping him between us.

His strained chuckle assures me that I've won. "Ye're a feisty woman, Lux Trace." But he reneges, finally, pressing me forward and up so when I return to his lap, he slides deep inside me. The pressure of him, particularly at this angle, steals my breath. I close my eyes, reveling in the feel of him, deep and thick, then open them to the curious gaze across from me. As I channel my energy into movement, I focus on her, and the erotic tension drives me down on Fin's cock again… and again.

When exquisite waves crash over me, Fin begins to shudder with his own release. And I watch with appreciation as the woman does as well, her lover pushing her over the edge. I collapse against Fin, and he wraps his arms around me, his warmth easing the chill creeping over my bare skin.

I must have dozed off, because when I'm aware of my surroundings again, Fin is gazing down at me with a smile. "Hello, beautiful."

With a small grin, I curl against him. "I have a problem."

"What's that?"

"If we're ever to go home, I'll have to figure out how to get back into my costume."

He glances around at the now packed room with every possible sexual position on display. "I doubt anyone would notice if I take ye out to the car just as ye are, love." His brows draw together in puzzlement as he stares across the room. "How did he get her into that position…" He cocks his head to the side, then a little further. "Aye, I daresay we could both walk out of here ruttin' like deer, and no one would bat an eyelash."

"Tempting, but…" I glance about for my costume, but it's been trampled under a clutch of bodies.

He's already shrugging out of his shirt.

If any of the neighbors were peeking about, they might have wondered what was going on as a bare-chested, kilted Scotsman carried a laughing, barely dressed woman down the sidewalk.

Chapter 18
The Truth about Love

Love. It sweeps in and steals all logic. In its wake, it leaves desolation and grief. At least, that's how it's always seemed to me. After our wild night at the sex party, Fin took me home, and while I wanted him to stay, I didn't ask him to. Even though I think he wanted me to. I can't even say why I didn't. Perhaps it was the extreme intimacies we'd shared that night, or the conflicting emotions that seem to define my inner thoughts as of late. Whatever it was, something stopped me from inviting him in, and so I spent yet another lonely night in my bed.

It's been three days. We've exchanged some texts, but when he's tried to turn up the heat, I've withdrawn. I can't explain it. Or maybe I don't want to. My gut aches with longing, and all I want to do is run to him. What I do instead is focus on business. I have two new clients to initiate, regular clients to keep happy, and plenty of things to think about when it comes to Kinked. I promised myself that I wouldn't sleep with anyone but Fin since our first date, but the familiar longing for something, anything, to break through the intense ball of emotion inside builds.

All of which is stupid because if I'd just get over my issues and call him, this wouldn't be a problem. Instead, I wallow in my fear, knowing that I should get past it, but refusing to budge.

Fin doesn't suffer from the same reticence, however.

Noah glances over at me where I'm lying across the couch reading a romantic thriller. "You wanna go out? Maybe grab some food and drinks?"

I lower my book and consider his offer. "I don't think so. Maybe another night. But I'm kind of 'done' for today. I spent three hours on a Skype call with Divine's marketing witch. I'm really, really over her."

He laughs. "She does seem to have it in for you."

"That's putting it mildly. The bitch essentially treats me like the hired help, as though this isn't my idea and life's blood," I growl, which sounds comical even to me. "She annoys the shit out of me."

He eyes me suspiciously. "Still…you haven't seen Fin in several days because you've been home early almost every night… and you don't want to go out and blow off some steam after a long day?" He presses steepled fingers to his lips. "What's going on?"

I roll my eyes in what I hope is a convincing way. "Nothing. Just taking a break."

"Did you guys break up?"

I don't answer for a few seconds. "I don't think so."

"You don't *think* so? What's going on, Lulu?"

I dog-ear the page of my book, then stare at the ceiling, trying to figure out what to say. Then I give up. "I told him I love him."

Noah nods. "And?"

"He told me he loves me too."

"And this is a problem… why?"

I shrug a shoulder. "Because I'm a commitment phobe? Because I ruin relationships? Because I'm incapable of doing things like this right? Take your pick."

He watches me for several minutes, as though waiting for me to say something else. But I don't. I continue to examine the ceiling for cracks, not really seeing anything in front of me, but rather, viewing the chaos inside my mind that surrounds my emotions. And I know it's an excuse. These are all pathetic excuses that I use to avoid dealing with the gooey parts of relationships.

"Look, I'm the worst person to ever give relationship advice—"

"So don't." I sit up. "Seriously, Noah, I know I'm being stupid. Fin's amazing—he's what every girl wants. More than that, even. But I fuck up relationships. It's what I do."

His brows draw together in annoyance. "So stop doing that."

The simplicity of his statement is like a blow to the gut. I want to respond, but the truth of it is the wakeup call I needed. A slow grin spreads across my face. "I guess I should, huh?"

Unsure, he nods. "Yeah, you should."

I drop my head in my hand, laughing. "God, I'm so fucked up."

"Can't argue with you there." But he says it with a small smile.

The doorbell rings, and he heads for it. Then he calls my name.

Fin is standing there, jeans and t-shirt covered in grime from a day of work.

"I'll let you guys to it," Noah mumbles before disappearing into the house.

I indulge in the sight of Fin, his skin burnished from the sun and his eyes fiery with frustration.

"Is there a reason ye're avoiding me? Did I do something wrong?" Hands on hips, his accent twists the words so I can barely make them out.

"No, you didn't. I did."

That takes the wind out of his very puffed up sails. "So. Were ye planning on telling me that? Or talking to me again at all?"

"I was. I am. I meant to. I just..." I sound like an idiot. "I love you."

"Aye. I love ye too. I told ye that." And the light bulb goes on. "That's why I havena heard from ye, isn't it?"

I raise my eyebrows with a tense smile. "That's me. Romance killer of the year. I have a wall *full* of trophies."

His shoulders drop as he looks at me for a moment, as though trying to understand what makes me tick. "Ye're not broken, Lux. Hurt, maybe. A little bruised. But ye aren't falling to pieces, love."

His kindness nearly undoes me, so rather than let emotions take their course, I pull his head down to mine and kiss him with all the insecurity and fear that's welled inside of me, as though I can excise them by drinking him in.

He grabs my arms, pushing me back. "Love, I'm a mess. Ye dinna want to get that close to me."

And there is definitely a distinct horse-y odor. "You need a shower."

He grins. "Aye, I do."

I take his hand and pull him into the house. Noah returns to the living room, so we escape upstairs.

He insists on rinsing himself off before letting me into the shower with him. I admire his naked form through the fogged glass until he opens the door for me to join him. I lather him with soap, paying close attention to his most intriguing bits, until he's straining with need. He pulls me to him, sheathing himself in one stroke. We move together, mouths exploring, hands seeking, finding each other without words. He presses me into the wall, my legs clasped around his waist, and holds me tight as I shake against him, unsure if I'm remade or broken.

He traces small hearts and circles over my breasts and stomach as he lies beside me in bed. "I had to see ye. When ye dinna respond to my last message, I feared ye might have been angry at me."

I shake my head in disbelief. "For what? Being too perfect?"

He raises an eyebrow, then snorts. "I dinna think that, no."

I meet his beautiful gaze, unable to stop myself from admiring his strong jaw covered in late-day shadow. I run a finger over his reddish whiskers, enjoying the texture. "Well, you are five years younger than me."

He makes a face. "Does that truly bother ye? It's not like I can change my age."

"When I'm thirty, you will be twenty-five."

He looks about the room, then back at me. "And...?"

"Nothing." I can feel myself turning pink. "It's stupid. I've just never been with someone younger before." I shrug.

He nods. "I've never been with someone older, but I haven't noticed that it's been an issue. Have ye?"

I stick my tongue out at him and bury my face in my pillow, my cheeks hot in embarrassment.

"Well then." He waits a beat. "What's the real issue?"

I look away, wishing I wasn't so abominable at love. "I've never really felt like this about someone. I mean, I've thought I was in love, but there were always games being played. I always knew I was safe. I couldn't really get hurt. But with you," I force myself to face him, "I could."

"Aye, and it goes both ways, love." He shifts to his stomach, his thigh aligning with mine. "Ye have the same power over me." He holds his hand out to me as we lie side by side.

I slip my fingers through his, trace the flat of his palm as I try to figure out what is really niggling at me. "That doesn't bother you?"

He watches me curiously. "It's part of the deal. When ye love someone, ye hold both parts of them in yer hands—the good and the bad. Ye could hurt me, sure, but being with ye makes my world a better place. Ye remind me why I have ambitions and goals, why I want to be the best at what I do. Because ye do that every day in yer own life." He feathers a kiss over my knuckles. "This isn't just about having fun in bed, Lux. I enjoy making love with ye, of course. But even more so, I admire ye and yer vision. And I love that ye always take time to recognize the needs in others and help them come to terms with them. That's what made me fall in love with ye in the first place."

Only the sound of the air conditioning hums in the room. I stare at the ceiling, at a loss for words. No one's ever said anything like that to me before. I feel raw, a bit too open, and I don't know how to respond.

After a few minutes, his fingers flit over my side, and I shriek with laughter and curl away from him. He doesn't give in, tickling me until I launch myself at him, pinning him to the bed.

"Knew I could get ye where I wanted ye." He holds my hips, pressing himself against me.

"Just like a man. Only after one thing," I tease, jerking my head back when he tries to kiss me.

Without warning, he gathers me to him and flips us over. "Aye, just like a man, eh?" He nips my breast.

I yelp in surprise, then narrow my eyes at him. "Oo, payback is going to be a bitch."

"Only if ye can tie me down again with your wee ropes, love. Otherwise, I'm going to take what's mine," he threatens, biting my other breast lightly.

I'd argue further, but the pressure of his cock against me feels incredible, and I'd much rather focus on that.

He isn't quite finished. A serious look on his face, he toys with a lock of my hair. "Ye're right, Lux. I am after only one thing." His hand caresses my cheek, his gaze penetrating my soul. "You."

The purity of his words leave me with a lump in my throat, so rather than try to respond, I pull his face to mine, once again hoping I can convey with my kiss everything I wish I could say. I shift beneath him, spreading my legs so he can come into me fully. He holds my face, his gaze unwavering as he maintains a slow rhythm. Even when my breath falters and comes in gasps, he stares deep into me as though he can see through the shadows and anguish into the darkest corners. When he finally kisses me, it's as though I've been stripped naked, only this time on the inside, and whatever he found was exactly what he sought.

After, when we're both sweaty and satisfied, he holds me against him. "I love ye, Lux," he whispers as he drifts off to sleep.

But I can't sleep. While my desire is sated, my hunger for him scares me. I've never *needed* anyone before in my life. My determination to be self-sufficient has driven me for a long time. Undoubtedly, it's why I've had very few relationships that went past the first couple of weeks. While a little over a month hardly constitutes a long-term relationship, my feelings for Fin suggest that I'm falling for him like I've never fallen for anyone. I want to be happy about this, but a gut-deep fear niggles at the edges.

While I've never been hardcore BDSM in my own sex life, I do control the environment. I've always been the top. I can enjoy vanilla sex, and certainly, I relish making love with Fin. But with him, there's much more give and take than I'm used to. And on one hand, it's refreshing to be with someone who's just into me for me, and not what I can do for or to them. I've never been involved in something like this before. What if it doesn't last? What if I can't have a long-term relationship like this? What if I get bored?

What if he wants children and a stable life with that white picket fence? That's not who I am, and as I watch him sleep, his face relaxed and innocent, I can't help but believe that he deserves a chance at that. He's twenty-three, and he hasn't even finished college yet. I was an idiot when I was twenty-three and just starting to find my footing as a Dom.

Not to mention, what if he doesn't get into the local college? What if he has to go home? The idea of a long distance relationship doesn't thrill me.

But the idea of losing him…terrifies me. I reach out, running my fingers over his forehead and cheek. The corner of his mouth turns up reflexively, but he remains sound asleep. I am in love with this gorgeous, kind, and passionate man…but doesn't loving someone involve wanting the best for them? What if I can't give him that? Or worse, what if I get in the way of it?

Chapter 19
Family Matters

The next morning, Fin joins Noah and me at the table for coffee and the newspaper perusal. I washed his work clothes last night, so he smells like laundry detergent.

Noah quickly excuses himself. "Ella is determined to start jogging, and I'm pretty sure if I don't show up, it'll never happen." He drops a kiss on my head, shares a manly bumping of fists with Fin, and then it's just the two of us.

He's reading the international news, sipping his over-creamed coffee—"You Americans and yer bitter drinks; I'll never understand ye"—and I occasionally glance over. What would it be like to do this every morning? Wake up to his sunny disposition, which never seems to wane, make lazy love first thing, as we did this morning, and then share coffee and the paper…I'm finding myself warming to the idea, which is a surprise, particularly after my tempestuous thoughts last night.

I don't realize he's meeting my gaze until he reaches for my hand. "Ye've got a bit of a smile on yer face, love. Penny for yer thoughts?"

That makes me laugh. "God, people still say that?" When he looks rightfully annoyed, I chuckle a bit more. "Sorry, my grandfather used to say that when I was little. I never really understood why he'd give me a penny, when no one else offered."

"So ye'll mock me for being old-fashioned, or Scottish, eh?" He pretends irritation.

I stand, then swing myself over his lap, straddling him. He leans back so he can look at me. "Can I ask ye something?"

"Sure." I kiss him, though, before he can. My ebullient mood seems limitless at the moment, and it's been a long time since I've felt this way.

Eventually, though, he pulls away, extracting my arms from around his neck, laying them on his chest with his large, warm palms on top. "Why do ye not talk about yer family? I get the impression it's a source of pain for ye, and I dinna wish to make it worse. But I'd like to understand, at least."

I look away, down at the neckline of his v-neck t-shirt, then I swallow, trying to figure out how to answer him. "Let's just say…my family isn't like yours. I don't have warm memories of holidays or high school graduations." I avoid his gaze for fear of the pity I'll see there. "My family isn't like that, and I don't like to talk about them." I kiss him, then gently extract myself under the guise of putting dishes in the dishwasher and refilling coffee cups.

He comes to stand behind me, pulling me back into him. The top of my head fits neatly under his chin. "I'm sorry, Lux. I dinna mean to upset ye."

I close my eyes, inhaling deeply. The scent of him eases the ache in my chest, and I turn in his arms. "It's not your fault. And I'm not upset. It's just hard to explain to people." I give him a peck, then stand back and admire him. "And unless I miss my guess, we haven't played mini-golf together yet."

He arches an eyebrow. "Mini-golf, eh?"

"This must be remedied, immediately."

I run upstairs to change into sneakers and jeans, but in the back of my mind, I know I'm doing more of the same—what I do in every relationship.

Avoid.

Make excuses.

Refuse to be vulnerable.

And deep down, I know I will destroy this if I don't stop myself.

Later that night, after we've gorged on sushi and Ben and Jerry's (Chunky Monkey for Fin, Cherry Garcia for me), and long after the credits roll on the movie we rented, I find myself relaxed in his arms. I don't realize he's asleep until I hear his soft snore. It's all I can do not to laugh, but I move carefully, just enough so I can look at him. In repose, his ginger eyelashes mimic the curve of his cheek, his full bottom lip slightly pouting. Even so, he appears content. Happy, even. I know from the times we've talked that he has a wonderful family, very supportive, and he talks to them often.

I run my hand along his arm gently. He stirs a bit, but then his patterned breathing resumes. His warmth reassures me, though I'm not sure why. He's so solid, I guess. He knows what he wants in life, and he never wavers. God, I admire that. I wonder if I would have been more like that, had I grown up in a stable family with warmth and love. These musings offer nothing good, so I snuggle back down against him. But I can't sleep. Not as thoughts roll across my mind, about Kinked, about the complications whirling around Fin and my relationship, about life in general.

"I dozed off," he says sleepily after an hour or so has passed. He stretches, then gazes down at me with a satisfied sigh. "I rather like waking up to ye twice in a row."

I wiggle up so I can kiss him. "You hang out much longer, you'll do it for a third time in the morning."

He checks the clock. "Dammit. I should get going. I dinna think ye'll want my 4:30 alarm."

I make a face of horror. "Most certainly not."

But there's a hollow in my heart as he gathers his few things and puts his shoes on. At the door, he pulls me into his arms, and I breathe him in, my hands trailing into his silky hair, the slightly salty taste of his neck as I press my mouth to him.

"I dinna want to leave ye." He kisses me for probably the twelfth time, but I'm not complaining.

A smile blooms from deep inside, and even my doubts can't diminish it. "I wish you didn't have to."

"Tomorrow night?"

I picture my day planner in my mind's eye. "I think I'm finished around 9 p.m."

He captures my mouth in a searing kiss, which I take as an affirmative response.

"Any chance ye'll let me tie ye up with yer ropes, love? A little 'turnabout is fair play'?"

My stomach races for my toes, but I think about what Charles said, about not really knowing your position until you've experienced others, and my own worries from the evening before. If I'm going to make this work with Fin, maybe I need to be more flexible. "Okay. One night. And you'll never breathe a word about it to anyone."

His mouth is the only response I get, and I'm a puddle of aroused goo when the door closes behind him.

Noah and I are digging into a spreadsheet for project expenses for Kinked. While I want to do this, I hate imposing on him when I know he's knee-deep in work, but he insisted it was okay. We've spread out to the small brick patio in front of the brownstone, and the temperature is mild enough to require a light sweater.

When my phone dings with the text message, Noah rolls his eyes. "God save me from the sexting."

"You're just jealous," I say as I grab my phone out of my back pocket.

If you had any idea what I intend to do to you tonight…

I can't believe how turned on I'm getting over the idea of being held captive to this man. The tingle of desire has me vibrating, but I try to hide it from Noah.

Mmm. Sounds yummy. Of course, you'll have me at a disadvantage. What will you use for a gag, I wonder?

"Can we get back to the timeline estimates now?" Noah acts irritated, but there's a glint of humor in his yes.

"Yessir." I nod.

We've nearly got a full timeline with costs written out, and we're starting on the spreadsheet calculations when my phone vibrates again.

"I'm getting a beer." Noah smiles falsely down at me and says in a sing-song voice. "Do you want one?"

I can't help myself. I giggle. "I'm good. But you do that. I'll be right here, discussing lascivious sex plans with my lover."

With that, he mock gags and goes in the house.

I'll have to use my cock for that, I suppose. I might have to borrow your tools. Surely you have a few things I might find intriguing.

My cheeks heat up. I have several I can think of off the top of my head. One of them being that new vibrator…

Well, a professional *should* bring his own toys, but I guess I can make an exception. But only if you promise to make me come several times.

I hope Fin's not at the barn, because he's likely hard as a rock after this conversation.

Noah returns with his beer, and he mixed me a peach martini.

"Aw, tank you!" I say sweetly, enjoying the sharp tang of the liquor.

I intend to have you crying out my name many, many times tonight.

I shake my head, catching Noah's eye and laughing at his expression. "Hey, you want me happy or cranky? You choose."

He smiles. "Always happy, Lulu."

Promises, promises.

Chapter 20

Bound

Because I'm not the one in the driver's seat tonight, I go with a more low-key outfit. Gone are the corset and leather thigh boots, garters and nylons. I opt for a short, spaghetti-strap sundress, with a modest emerald bikini and strapless bra set, along with bare feet. My hair is in long ringlets, its natural state, and I keep my makeup minimal, with just a bit of mascara and blush. Of course, I'm pretty sure I could be naked, and Fin would be just as happy.

The look on his face when I answer the door makes it all worth it.

"Dear Christ, Lux, ye're beautiful." He stands there for a moment, admiring me, and I preen under the attention. "Come to me."

So it begins.

He draws me to him like a magnet regardless, so there's no hesitance when I step into his arms. He holds me, rubbing my back. I feel like Nellie, having bucked and fought, and now I'm turned towards him, ready to be part of whatever comes next.

His kisses are slow, without eroticism, though that makes them even more so. His palms travel the length of my sides, sliding beneath my dress.

"We should go inside," he whispers, his fingers teasing over my panties.

"*Aye*," I answer, breathless.

Upstairs, I've laid out everything I have that I'd want used on me, which was a tough decision to begin with. While I've always imagined what certain things would feel like—a hearty spanking or a well-placed crop strike—I've never allowed it to happen. Now that I am…I don't know what I like. I leave it up to him.

"So." He looks around the room, scratching the back of his neck for a moment. "I guess…we should have ground rules, yes?"

I sit down on my bed, flattening my dress modestly against my thighs. "This is your scene. You get to set it up." My pulse quickens with both desire and nerves.

He snorts. "Aye, well, I rather like it when I get to just lie back and enjoy." He grins then, his dimple enhancing his charm. "Let's see… ye dinna need to call me 'Master' or anything like that. And I dinna wish to call ye slave or some such names."

I snicker. "Did your research, did you?"

He nods. "For weeks now. Found a book called something like…" He thinks for a moment. "*Screw the Roses, Send me the Thorns?*"

"Yes, that's a great reference. Particularly for a beginner," I praise him. Though given some of the things they outline in its pages, he might have gotten some ideas…

He beams. "Fascinating wee book." He holds up his hands, showing me its thickness, or rather, lack thereof. "Learned quite a bit."

"Hm." I drop my chin and gaze up at him.

His tone turns from academic curiosity to lust in barely a second. He crosses to the bed, hauling me against him and kissing me hard.

"I believe I'll leave the finer elements of BDSM to ye, Mistress Hathaway, but for tonight, ye'll be mine to do with as I wish. Am I clear, love?" He bends to my neck, his teeth grazing the skin.

"Very."

"And ye'll come when I say, and not before." He draws a hot path along my collarbone, nudging my dress strap out of his way.

"Yessir," I agree, my head falling back as his mouth seeks lower, stopped only by the neck of my dress.

"And I did bring a surprise for ye."

I raise an eyebrow as he pulls something out of his rear jeans pocket. "Oh really? I can't wait to see."

He hands me a finely crafted handcuff set. The leather cuffs are soft as butter and held together by a buckle. I admire the deep shade of the hide, even as my insides lurch at the idea of being confined in them. "These weren't cheap."

"Well, ye said I should bring my own tools, so I stopped by Shay's on my way here."

"Fair enough."

He takes them from me and draws me against him. "Are ye okay with this, love? We don't have to do it tonight if ye're having second thoughts."

His eyes—nearly green in the low light—search mine for an answer, so I close my eyes and kiss him. "I am yours tonight."

When my hands are tethered to the bed frame, I feel a bit less confident about that answer. He opted to keep the cuffs hooked together and looped over one of the headboard's rods, so my wrists are comfortably bound directly above my head. Fin's gaze studies me as though he wishes to memorize every detail, and my sex drive revs to life. He runs a slow hand over my leg, his fingers stopping just shy of my panties.

"I must admit: I had a plan in mind, but now that I'm here, all I want to do is worship at yer feet, love." His gaze, molten and hungry, locks onto mine, and I can't look away. "Do ye know how stunning ye are? How much I want to lose myself in ye?"

I swallow, moisture pooling between my legs. I have no idea what to say, as I'm desperate for his touch. The intensity of my arousal scares me a bit. Why is this such a turn on for me?

When he slips a blindfold over my eyes, all my thoughts scatter. A sense of panic accosts me, but I push it away, determined not to ruin this for him. For several moments, I can't feel or hear him, and the anxiety rises. I shove down a threatening scream and listen for any movement. Then his belt buckle jangles, signaling its removal, and I relax slightly.

"Did ye really want me to use all of these on ye?" He sounds a bit incredulous, and he must be reviewing the items I left on the dresser.

His doubt eases my tension, and I consciously soften my limbs, trying to work out the rigidity. "Not all of them, no. But I wanted to give you options, in case there was something you wanted to try."

"Mmphmm." He sounds like he's deciding, and I hear a rustle of something. Then the bed dips with his weight.

His mouth makes me jump, his tongue sweeping into mine. He kisses me so thoroughly, I'm breathless. He blazes a path down my chest, taking advantage of my bra's front closure. My breasts freed, he captures a nipple, but at the same time, his knuckles spread my thighs. The telltale thrum of a vibrator sounds, and while he laves my sensitive nipples, he presses the vibrator against me. I arch my back as he slips past the edge of my panties, centering the bullet at the underside of my clit.

"Fuck," I breathe, jerking against him, but his legs hold mine captive.

"Come for me, Lux," he urges. His teeth scrape against my breast, and my whole body burns brighter. When I come, the world splits in two, and it's only Fin's weight and the cuffs that keep me anchored to the bed. I'm shaking, but he gathers me to him, holding me until my breath calms.

There's not much break before he takes possession of my mouth, his hand traveling south. When his fingers spread me, I struggle against the bonds, the intensity almost too much. "I can't…" But then I bite my lip as his fingers press into me, dancing against my center. "Oh, God, Fin, I don't think I can…"

He trails kisses over my jaw. "Ye can, love, just relax into it."

When he settles between my thighs, I'm already quaking, on the brink of climax. He pauses, not touching me for a minute.

I nudge my hips towards him. I want to feel his mouth on me. To be completely unable to do anything but react to the waves of pleasure that are gathering. To think of nothing more than my own bliss.

He offers me no response for long beats. Then I feel his breath blow over me. "What do ye want, Lux Trace?"

Oh God. He's going to make me ask. He teases me with a finger, briefly, and then…nothing. Dammit.

"What do ye want, love?"

I grit my teeth, wishing I could refuse, but I'm so desperate for his touch, I can't hold out. "I want you to touch me." I force out the next word. "Please."

"Is that all?"

God damn him. "I want you to make me come. Please."

I don't need to be able to see him to know he's got that crooked smile on his face right at this moment.

His tongue makes delicious designs on my hypersensitive folds, and when his fingers slip back inside me, I lose the ability to care. With whimpers and moans I barely recognize as my own, I teeter on the edge, only to fall off the cliff and into pure sensation. Fin doesn't let up, and I'm unable to do anything else but hang on as the waves crash over me.

My head lies on his shoulder as he rubs feeling back into my hands. "My throat's sore," I say.

"Aye, and no wonder. I'm pretty sure the neighbors could hear your lusty cries."

Free of the blindfold, I glance up at him, catching his smug smile, then snuggle back into him. "That's all your fault."

His chest rumbles beneath my cheek as he chuckles.

Silence thickens the air before I speak again. "Why didn't you fuck me?"

He shifts so I'm on my back, his arm coming around me to cup my ass and press me into him. "I was going to. But I changed my mind. Much as I loved seeing ye helpless and naked, I'd rather have ye powerful and commanding me as is yer wont, riding my cock before the night is over."

I blow out a breath and close my eyes. "I don't think that's going to happen. I'm exhausted." My legs feel like overcooked noodles.

He smiles, then brushes his lips against mine. "I'll do all the work."

I pop open one eye. "You'd be having your way with an unconscious woman."

He looks mildly offended. "That sounds unappealing." He's appraising me closely when I drop my eyelid back down.

When he gives up and lies on his back, I can't ignore him any longer. "Where's your fight, man? You aren't letting me off the hook that easily, are you?"

"Ye said ye're exhausted. What kind of man am I if I push you?"

I roll my eyes. "You're the one in charge tonight, remember? I am at your command." I raise an eyebrow in challenge.

He gazes at me for a long moment, before a grin curves his lips. "Aye, then, woman. Get on my cock."

I'm pretty sure I don't move all night. When Fin spoons me sometime after sunrise, I barely register him until his cock enters me from behind. I'm sore from an extended session of fucking wherein I came at least three more times, bringing yesterday evening's orgasm total to six…maybe seven? Despite the discomfort, his oh-so-knowing hands arouse me, and before I've even opened my eyes, I'm coming yet again.

"I'm pretty sure this has set an all-time record for me where orgasms are concerned," I tell him afterwards. I'm snuggled into his chest as he lies on his side, propped up and gazing down at me.

He smiles. "The least I could do, for letting me have my way with ye." His finger traces my hairline, then down my nose to my lips. "I have to tell ye something."

My stomach flips over on itself. "That sounds ominous."

His face turns serious. "Aye, well, I'm not particularly happy about it, no." He pauses, then continues. "I'm going away for a few weeks. John has a few out of state clients; he'd like me to go along."

I stare at his chest, if only to avoid showing him how much this affects me. I take a deep breath. "Sounds like a great opportunity. How long will you be away?"

His hand slides over my arm, resting on my shoulder. "He canna say—several weeks at least."

I nod. "It sounds like a great opportunity for you. And he trusts you enough to let you join him."

"Aye, it is. I'm glad for it. But I'll miss ye." His finger follows a light path over my collarbone.

"You'll have to send me a postcard." I put on a good show of being unaffected, but inside, my heart aches at the thought.

When he leaves later that morning, his kiss has a sense of urgency to it, of parting, but I paste a smile on my face, go through the motions of being fine with everything.

"I'll call ye once we've arrived—we're dropping a horse off on the way, so it's likely to be a few days."

"That's fine."

He doesn't seem to know how to leave or how to handle my lack of response. I want to make it easier on him, tell him I'll miss him. But the words don't come, and he's long gone by the time the first tear falls.

Chapter 21

Burning

Time drifts by slowly when all you want is for it to fly. It's more than twenty-four hours since I've heard from Fin, and I'm a mess. And not because I miss him. Okay, that's a lie. It's part of it. I've never needed anyone, and I'm not about to let that change, dammit. Even though I find myself checking my phone every few minutes, waiting on a text message that doesn't come. *He's working,* I tell myself. *He's probably driving right now.* The conflict raging inside plunges me even deeper into shadows. What the hell has happened to me? When did I become a woman who waited around like a lovesick teenager? The idea of not seeing him for an indeterminate amount of time leaves me bereft and cranky.

Just as irksome: when did I turn into someone who *liked* getting tied up? I set the scene. I do the restraining. I sure as hell don't get turned on by some guy acting all alpha male on me and making me beg for an orgasm.

Yet that's exactly what happened. And more than that, I catch myself wondering what it would be like if it happened again.

I feel like a fraud. What kind of Dom am I? How the hell did this happen?

How do I fix it?

"Hey, Lulu, your phone just went off."

I glance up from my computer. "What? Oh. Just leave it."

Noah's in the kitchen making lunch, and his footsteps announce his return. "You sure? It's from Fin. Sounds like he's pretty worried."

The modern smartphone has destroyed all semblance of privacy. I snatch the phone from him, unlocking and relocking it to erase the message from the lock screen. But I can't avoid seeing it.

Lux, I don't know what's wrong. Can you at least let me know that you're okay?

Noah watches me closely, but when I don't look up at him, he takes the hint. A few minutes later, he tucks a grilled cheese panini with pesto tortellini and sautéed mushrooms—a favorite dish of mine from one of our local delis—by my elbow. "Wow. This looks amazing." And it smells even better.

I'm sitting at Ella's desk, using the brand new MacBook she and Noah talked me into buying—a business expense, they called it. Whatever it is, I'm enjoying it immensely, though I'm supposed to be working on research for Kinked's marketing plan.

"So what's the deal?"

Noah's penetrating gaze won't give me any peace, so I give in and turn to look at him. "What's what deal?"

He narrows his eyes at me.

I flick a glance at the ceiling with a long sigh. "There's no deal. Fin's out of town."

"And he's worried because you're not responding to his texts." He waits a beat. When I don't say anything, he prods. "Why?"

I've conveniently shoved very hot cheese and bread in my mouth, so it gives me plenty of time to avoid answering. Soon, I'm out of stall tactics. "Because I just haven't. I'm not…cut out for this."

His brows draw together. "You said you loved him."

If I hadn't felt adequately awful, I do now. "I know. I do. But this isn't…I don't know how to deal with this. People going away, missing them, feeling a bit adrift…" I lift a shoulder. "I'll talk to him about it when he gets back."

His concerned look turns to irritation. "And women say men suck at communication. The guy is worried about you, Lux. You should at least tell him you're okay. Please don't tell me he's tried to call you and you haven't answered."

I stare down guiltily at my plate, all appetite vanishing in the wake of my shame.

"Jesus. What the hell is wrong with you?" His voice escalates. "You've got some guy on the hook, believing that he's met the love of his life, and you treat him like this? How is this love?"

"How is this any of your business? Who made you the keeper of all appropriate behavior in relationships?" I shove back from the desk, slapping my laptop shut. "What I do or don't do is my affair." I grab my laptop and head for the stairs.

"Lux, this isn't like you. You don't fuck people over."

I spin around just as he's joining me in the hallway. "I am not fucking anyone over. I get that this isn't on your approved romantic decisions list. And I'm not saying I'm doing the right thing here. But it's not up to you to judge me or what I do. It's my choice, not yours. And given some of your own questionable indiscretions over the years, you are the *last* person I would expect to get high and mighty."

"*I* am not telling people I love them and then turning a cold shoulder the minute they're out of view. I don't lead anyone on with suggestions that there could be a future with me." He takes a step towards me, his voice intense and angry, and even though I'm furious, I can also hear the hurt beneath it. "You have this guy by the balls, and all you're doing is squeezing harder. To what end? Do you want to destroy what could be a really good thing for you?"

"If I do, or if I don't, it's my business. Being roommates doesn't qualify you to be my judge or make comments on my personal life."

"You're right—it doesn't. Being your friend *does*. And you are fucking this up."

I glare at him. "Stay out of my personal business, Noah. I don't comment on your romantic exploits. Leave mine alone." I stomp up the stairs and slam my bedroom door.

Guilt has a raging temper, as it turns out.

Noah is gone the next morning, and I assume he took his work to Ella's house. I feel terrible about the night before. I should call him, text him—hell, even an email would suffice—and express my apologies. But at the moment, I'm tired. Of everything. Of feeling guilty, even though it's deserved. Of fucking up everything. Of living in fear and excitement over Kinked. So I make myself a deal: I'll give myself the next two hours to wallow, and then I'll try to make things right.

I pour a cup of coffee, put on an old Pixies album, and pull out the morning paper. Nothing seems amiss until I get to the national news section.

"Dating Service Sued in Largest Sexual Assault Case Ever Filed." My insides turn to mush. The article describes how a serial rapist used a dating site to find his victims, and though the site claims they had no knowledge of his behavior and pattern, the prosecuting attorney insists the case is rock solid against them.

If all of that wasn't bad enough, a small accompanying article details the rapist's kinky preferences. I'm still reeling from the news when my phone rings. I don't even have to look at the caller ID.

Nance is apologetic, explains that Divine, Inc. is still interested, but at this time, they need to step back and reevaluate their investments. Given that we haven't signed contracts yet, it's better if they wait until after the first of the year to make a commitment. Of course I understand, I say. I would feel the same way. And of course, I'll keep them posted on any new developments in the plan for Kinked, if I continue to move forward.

I don't feel anything when I lay my phone on the table, drop my head on my arms, and close my eyes. I'm barely conscious of going to the freezer for the bottle of vodka, and after several shots, I pass out on the red couch in the living room, oblivious to the time, what day it is, and most importantly, the hollow spreading throughout my insides.

It's been twelve days since Fin left, a week since I got the news from Divine, Inc. I've succeeded in ignoring the ache in my heart, the shortness of breath that catches me at odd times, and the weird silent truce Noah and I have unconsciously created, since I have yet to apologize for being an ass. I want to. I just don't know what happened to my words.

I focus on work, take on more clients than I should, and avoid, avoid, avoid. One advantage to New York City: people with alternative sexual preferences are drawn here like moths to the proverbial flame, so I can forget my problems for days at a time. I still haven't listened to Fin's voice messages, and the texts have stopped, which is almost more of a relief than a disappointment. But deep down, I'm lost without him.

When Stephen calls with an invite to hang out at Paddled, I nearly leap at the chance. Anything to get out of this funk, to feel something besides the weighing darkness. With an energy I didn't know I possessed, I dig out my favorite club outfit: two leather swatches held together by muted crimson laces, masquerading as a micro-mini, a wine-colored satin corset with hand-embroidered roses, and stiletto knee-boots. My hair doesn't cooperate, so I leave it hanging in a mess of coils and make do with some anti-frizz spray.

Stephen meets me there.

"Look at you, dove." He steps back and whistles. "A sight for very sore eyes. And delicious, as well."

There's a flirtation in his voice that I have to admit I've missed. I offer him the first real smile I've managed in weeks. "As do you. I like the new look." Stephen is always reinventing himself, and tonight he donned skinny jeans and a dark angora sweater that fits his narrow, muscular frame like a glove.

We've been going to Paddled since we were twenty-one (despite the lack of alcohol, Paddled maintains an over twenty-one policy). When we walk in the door, the bouncer recognizes us and lets us through without comment. The music has a mystical quality this evening, though the small dance floor hears only its bass. I glance around, taking in the current pleasures, but despite my determination not to think about him tonight, Fin weighs heavy on my mind.

Stephen brings me a drink, standing a touch too close. "Watching or playing tonight, dove?" he whispers in my ear.

I purse my lips, considering his question as I sip my cranberry and soda. "I'll probably just watch."

"Probably?" His eyebrow arches, and he smiles coquettishly. "That sounds like the possibility for naughtiness isn't off the table."

With a quelling look, I head towards the stairs. I like Stephen as a friend, and while we've dallied in the same scenes together before, I'm not looking for anything remotely sexual tonight. But then…why did I say "probably"?

My phone vibrates in my small bag, but I don't look. If it's work or friend-related, I don't want to know. On the off chance it's Fin…I don't want to know that either. All I desire is to embrace the strange numbness that mutes my thoughts this evening.

It's well over an hour later when I feel a hand on my shoulder, the warmth of it flooding my body with hope. I turn, but the face isn't one I recognize. At least, not right away.

"Lux?"

There are two people standing beside me, actually. Then it hits me. "Josh, Mona, how cool to see you guys." I hug them eagerly. "It's been years. How's it going?"

Mona, a stunning brunette, smiles warmly. "Really well. The kids are finally sleeping through the night, so we can get out of the house."

Josh nods. "I barely recognize anyone here anymore."

Three or four years ago, Josh and Mona were standbys at Paddled. Mona loves being spanked, and Josh enjoys dominating her in any way she enjoys. I used to play with them on occasion, in wanton affairs involving kink and sensuality. For a long time, I was very attracted to both of them, so having sex with either or both of them was even more fun.

"You look exactly the same, Lux," Mona says after observing me closely. Her grin is seductive in a way that is so Mona.

I return the look. "You as well. Motherhood definitely agrees with you."

"Hm, well, I'm glad to finally be able to get back to things I enjoy." She squeezes Josh's arm.

He looks at me, turning a bit bashful. "We were going to head home—the kids won't sleep past six in the morning, so late nights are still not a possibility. But…we'd be open to having you join us for the evening."

Any other time, I'd jump at the opportunity. To enjoy a sexual romp with two people I find wildly attractive…where do I sign up? Even though I still feel the old pull and would like nothing better than to be distracted by two beautiful people, my insides long for something else. I shake my head. "I wish I could. I'm not in a good place for that right now."

"Ah, sweetie, is everything okay?" Mona lays her hand on my arm.

I nod. "Yeah, I'm fine. Just in a bad head space."

Josh squeezes my shoulder. "We know what that's like."

"Let me walk you out."

We catch up on the way out of the club, Mona gushing over their two-year-old while Josh admits to being wrapped around his three-year-old daughter's finger.

On the sidewalk, Josh hugs me, his hand lingering at my waist for just a moment. I'm surprised when Mona kisses me, but the contact feels wonderful, so I don't push her away. It's tantalizing, and they've always been very physical people, Mona especially.

As we say our final goodbyes, I hear a deep voice behind me. "I guess I can see why ye havna been returning my calls."

Chapter 22

Out of Bounds

I turn on my heel, so stunned by his voice, I'm pretty sure my jaw drops open. "What are you doing here?"

"Waiting for ye." Fin's tone is harsh, turning his Scottish brogue dark and ferocious.

He wears jeans and a black sweater, and from where I stand, I can smell the spicy fragrance of his cologne combined with him that drives me crazy.

"How did you know I—"

"Stephen told me."

I'm not sure if I've been set up or not, though I have a sneaky suspicion the earlier text I ignored was from Stephen. The part of me that's excited to see him doesn't care. The other part of me wants to run as fast as I can in the other direction.

"Just tell me why. That's all I want to know. Was I just a fling for ye? A one night stand that ye got a bit carried away with?" Anger vibrates in his words, thickening his burr until I can barely understand him. Beneath the anger lies pain.

I bite my lip, refusing the emotions that coil in my gut. "I'm sorry, Fin. But I did warn you. I don't do relationships well."

"Aye, ye did warn me. But why? Because of our last night?"

Wrapping my arms around myself, I try to avoid the shiver that's not wholly caused by the cool night air. "You mess with my head, Fin. It's like…I know who I am. What I'm capable of. You make me want…

other things. Things that I shouldn't want."

"Bullshit. It's just sex, Lux. I ken that it's a power play in yer world. But whether ye want to top or bottom, or just try something new, there's nothing wrong with it. Ye've taught me that." He shoves his hands in his pockets. "It's not that. This is something more. Something you won't even admit to yourself."

The truth of his words slap me, but I dig in. "This is my career. It's not 'just sex.' I have a fucking reputation, not to mention—how long is all this going to last? How long are you going to stand by and be okay with my job, when you're jealous just seeing me with someone else when you don't even know the context?" I fling my hand out, gesturing towards where I'd been standing with Mona and Josh. I'm grasping at straws, anything to keep him at a distance as I feel my defenses caving in.

"Don't make it about that. I dinna give a shite whether you kiss some other woman—or man for that matter. Hell, I don't even ken what yer job is, whether ye sleep with people or not, but I've never said one word about it, have I?" He takes a step a closer. "I want to ken why ye push everyone away when they try to get close to ye. Ye're right—I am jealous, but not in the way ye think. I'm jealous of whoever it is that gets the truth from ye, rather than avoidance and silence. I've called ye twelve times. Twelve times! And texted ye more times than I can count. Ye'd think ye could at least let me know ye're okay. No, I have to get that information from Noah."

"Noah called you?"

"No, I called him. Just to make sure that ye were alive and not hurt in the hospital somewhere."

If I didn't feel like shit before (and I did), I'm beyond that now. "I'm sorry." I stare at his feet, the ground, anywhere but at the pained look on his face. "I'm sorry. You're right. I should have responded, at least to tell you I was okay." His stare bores into me, but I can't meet it. Coward, thy name is Lux Trace.

"Aye, ye should've." He blows out a breath and rakes his hands through his hair. "Are ye angry at me for tying you up? Do ye not trust me?"

I gnaw on the inside of my lip, but the tears burn my eyes regardless. "I don't trust anyone, Fin. It's not you. In this case, it really is all me."

His face is a mask of frustration and hurt. "That first night we were together, ye cried in my arms, Lux. And that last night… ye seemed to enjoy yerself. But then ye shut down… I want to know why. I ken that this is difficult for ye, and I think I even ken why, but there's things ye won't tell me, and it keeps me in the dark. What happened to ye?"

I hate him for asking, but even more than that, I hate myself. For not knowing what to do or how to fix the brokenness that destroys everything I touch. Tears stream down my cheeks, unchecked. I stare at the sidewalk, trying to sort through the damage inside and the wreck I'm making.

He reaches for me. "Lux, what is it? Ye can tell me."

I jerk back, away from comfort. After all I've put him through, I feel like I owe him this. "I have two sisters—we all have different fathers. My dad was a drug user, and he disappeared into that world. He overdosed when I was little. My mom could never pull her shit together. So my sisters and I…we ended up in foster care. And I was an angry kid, which I'm sure comes as no surprise.

"My last foster home wasn't a bad one, overall. I was the oldest there. The woman—we called her 'Mama C'—she was nice enough. Super religious, but she tried to be understanding. There were five of us: my sisters and two others much younger, so I took care of the kids a lot. Her husband, though…he wasn't as nice." Even if the air didn't carry a chill, I'd be freezing. Fin stands so close I could touch him if I reach out. He's a statue, listening.

"His brother lost his job and lived with us for almost two years. And one night, not long after he'd moved in… I was fifteen at the time and completely infatuated with him. He wasn't good-looking; at least, not what most people would call handsome. But he'd traveled, and he always had a funny story or a memory—he was a great storyteller. When he came onto me, I was flattered. It was sexy, I thought, that I was so young and he liked me. So one night, after everyone else had gone to bed, I snuck downstairs to talk to him. He offered me a beer. So I joined him, trying to act all grown up. And he started talking dirty. And it felt good, you know? It wasn't like abuse. It was sexy, and I felt attractive. When he started touching me, I wanted it." Emotion clogs my throat, making it hard to take a breath. Fin doesn't move, doesn't try to touch me, but I can see it takes everything in him not to do so.

"Mama C always told me to wait until I was married to have sex.

I was fifteen, Fin. I had a sex drive, hormones, desires—I just wanted to know what it was like. We made out, and he undressed me… kept telling me how beautiful I was and how much he had always liked me. I wanted it. Or, at least, I thought I did. But when he unbuttoned his pants, I got scared. This wasn't the way I wanted my first time to be, and the truth of what was about to happen terrified me. I tried to get away, but he was so far gone with alcohol, and I'd let him get that far, he was determined. So he pushed me down on the couch, on my back, and my arm was trapped beneath me. The way I was positioned, I couldn't move. And he fell on top of me, so heavy I couldn't take a breath."

Fin's gaze never leaves me, though his eyes have turned steely blue, and his nose flares a bit. Otherwise, he is still.

"Just when things were about to get really unpleasant, my foster father came downstairs. He caught us in the nick of time. Mama C was devastated. Of course, I got blamed. Not by her, but by *him*. And not in a violent or blatant way. In the most passive-aggressive, quiet way he could. It was always in his gaze, in sly comments when I'd break up with a boyfriend, or have problems in school. And his brother continued to live with us. I had a curfew in my own home—I had to be in my room before nine every night, just so I wouldn't be left unchaperoned because they let a monster live in that house. My sisters were there—they were eleven and thirteen at the time. So I stayed as long as I could, hoping that I could protect them. That's the way I lived, until I was seventeen. The brother ended up in prison for theft charges, which meant my sisters were safe from him. I moved out, and I never talked to any of them again."

A muscle in his jaw pulses as we both stand our ground.

"Lux, I'm so sorry."

Tears threaten again, and I brush them away, anger making my hands shake. "Yeah, well, it happened. And it's over. That's why I got upset the first time we were together. I couldn't move—my arm was trapped—and it freaked me out."

"Please let me hold ye. Don't make me stand here and watch ye cry."

The last thing I want is to yield, but his plea is nearly as pained as my own heart's. I barely nod before he's beside me, around me, holding me so tight that my sobs are lost between us.

It feels like hours until I can lift my head and wipe my eyes. His arms hold me together, and I lean into him, feeling his solid, constant presence like a balm to my wounds.

When I can meet his gaze, the love there steals my breath. His hands hold my head as his lips close on mine. His kiss is sweet and gentle, but I want neither. Pulling him into me, I assault his mouth, my hands sliding beneath his sweater and pulling his hips against mine. His hands squeeze my shoulders, and he pulls his face away. "Lux, what're ye—"

"Shut up."

His eyes gauge me, as though unsure, but when I grind my hips into him, he grabs my shoulders, crushing my mouth to his. His arms are bands of steel, locking me against him, but I shove away. There's a small alley between Paddled and the next building, just wide enough for two people to pass. I follow it, knowing that it leads to the back employee entrance for the club.

When I turn, Fin is there, hauling me up against him, his tongue sweeping inside my mouth. I bite his lip, earning an even tighter vise around my waist. His fingers tangle in my hair, forcing my head to the side so he can press his teeth against my neck. I inhale sharply, the pressure almost painful, but also incredibly erotic.

His hands grip my ass, his fingers pulling at the bottom of my short skirt.

I wrap my leg around his hips. "Fuck me."

"I aim to." He pushes me back against the brick wall. With rough hands, he reaches beneath my skirt and pulls my g-string down. I spread my legs wider as he kneels between my thighs. He eats me hungrily, teeth nipping and tongue insistent. The intensity rushes through me, my clit throbbing with need. When I come, my knees give out, and I span the wall with both hands to remain upright.

Fin stands, pants undone, cock hard and pulsing, and when he shoves inside of me, I can't even make a noise. He feels huge, and I wrap my legs around his waist, pulling him even deeper into me. He grips my ass as he pounds me, raw urgency turning us both into instinct driven creatures. Pure need draws us into a fast rhythm, and we use each other hard. When I come again, I'm hoarse as I cry out, and he buries his head in my neck as he shudders against me.

When he releases me to the ground, my legs shake. I pull my clothing back into place, unable to look at him. I step away, putting a few steps between us. He stands there, confusion evident in his furrowed brows.

The night air chills my overheated skin. "I want to be with you… so much. But I can't." Tears threaten, and I suck in air, trying to stymy their arrival. "You deserve better than this, Fin." I lay my hand against the wall, embarrassed by how aggressive our coupling was. "This isn't love. This is lust. I want you, but not enough to be open and be vulnerable with you. You need to be with someone who isn't a mess, and with someone who's ready to be as honest and wonderful as you are in a relationship." He opens his mouth to interrupt, but I rush to continue. "And it's not me. I haven't dealt with this shit. *Clearly*. And I need to." A lone tear escapes, but I brush it away. "I can't do this with you. And I'm sorry, because I'd like to. I just can't."

"Lux, what are ye saying?" He steps towards me, reaching out to touch my arm.

I retreat backwards, careful to avoid his hand. "I'm sorry. I'm so very sorry." I fight to keep my voice from shaking. "I need to figure things out. And I need to do it alone."

"I love ye."

In this moment, I know I am the worst human being alive. "I know. But I don't love you. I want to. I tried to love you. But I don't feel that way, even though I really wish I did. I'm sorry."

The knife buries deep, and his face wears the destruction.

I want to take it all back, to do something, anything, to comfort him. Instead, I turn and walk away. Tears course down my cheeks, and I keep walking until I'm in the club, in the bathroom, in the stall, before I break down completely.

Chapter 23
True Friends

I've never spent much time being lonely. In part, because I got used to being alone. There aren't many choices when you walk out of the only home you've ever known and never look back. The last few weeks since I broke up with Fin have been my first real experience feeling the darkness of being lost. I'm so desolate, I don't recognize myself in the mirror.

I don clothing, put on makeup. Wear the flirtatious—or evil—smile and do my job. But inside, there's nothing left. I'm an empty husk. Noah and Ella have stopped asking about Kinked. They've stopped asking much of anything, really. And I hide in my room most days, to avoid crossing paths with them.

I don't know how many weeks it's been, but eventually, Ella knocks on my bedroom door. "Lux? It's me."

When I don't answer, she opens the door. "Lux?" When she sees me, her expression tells me just how bad I look. "Oh my God."

I lift up on one elbow and shove my hair out of my face. "The door was closed."

"I know." Apparently my unfriendly tone of voice intimidates her for a moment. "Can I come in?"

"You're already 'in,'" I grumble, but then I relent and pat the bed. "Make yourself comfortable."

She sits on the bed, and when I don't bite, she lies down beside me. I fall back into my blanket nest, clutching a small pillow to my stomach.

Ella brings with her the citrusy scent of her favorite perfume. Given that I haven't showered in two days, I'm trying not to sniff too hard in the direction of my armpits.

"You and Fin broke up."

"Yep."

"Why?"

I toy with an answer, then go with the truth. "Because he deserves someone who will treat him with respect and love, not fuck with his head and keep him on edge."

She turns on her side, resting her head against her arm. "True."

When she doesn't say anything more, I breathe a sigh of relief. "Thank you for not arguing."

She snorts. "When you're right, you're right."

I manage a small grin. "I have my moments."

"You deserve all those things, too."

I direct my gaze out the window, evaluating the sun and what time it might actually be. "Not when I can't give them in return."

"Right, but you *could* give them in return, Lux. You just gotta figure out what's stopping you." She pauses. "Have you thought about talking to someone?"

I turn my gaze to her. "Like a shrink?"

"Like a therapist or counselor, yes." Her tone turns wry and knowing. "They aren't as scary as you think they are."

"How would you know?"

She sits up, crossing her legs in a yoga pose. "Because when I was pregnant, I started having some anxiety issues. Nothing major, and I knew it wasn't rational. I'm married to the best man ever who has done nothing but reassure me that he's just as committed to our family as I am. But I was nearly catatonic with anxiety some days. So I got some professional help."

"Why didn't you ever tell me?" I feel like the worst friend ever for not noticing.

"I didn't tell anyone. Not even Noah. I was embarrassed. I have everything—a beautiful home, a wonderful husband, a roaringly successful business. Why on earth would I have any issues at all? But I did. And I worked through them." She reaches for my hand. "And I'd like to see you get past this. Maybe there's still hope for you and Fin."

I shake my head. "No, I ruined that. Completely. He needs someone who deserves him, without all the baggage. Someone his own age."

"He didn't seem to mind the age difference."

"No, he never did. He wasn't even thrown off by what I do for a living. Or that I was sleeping with clients." I say it casually, as though she knew it the whole time.

Her eyes widen. "You what?"

I dig my palms into my eyes to avoid looking at her, as though I'm having a sudden flare of allergies. When I can't stall any longer, I look at her, but can't quite meet her gaze. "I was having sex with a few my clients. Not a bunch of them, but a couple. And I'm not proud of it. I'm embarrassed, actually, because I'm not a prostitute. If any of the other Doms found out, they'd destroy me publicly. And I'd deserve it. I broke all the rules that are in place for a reason."

She falls silent, turning her engagement and wedding rings around on her finger, over and over. "Are you still—"

"No." I clip off the word. "Not since I started dating Fin."

The faint hum of Noah using the copier downstairs is the only sound as we avoid looking at each other.

"You know I would never judge you for that. Please tell me you know that."

"I know." I examine my chipped nail polish. "But I judge me. And I'm not proud of it."

"You can get past this, Lux. And Kinked isn't over. I know it seems that way. But it's not."

I don't ask how she knows, but I'm pretty sure Noah's been opening some of my mail to make sure I don't miss a bill. Divine most likely sent a paper trail about their withdrawal. "For now, it is. It's not in me, and I'm not sure I really want that anyway."

She doesn't argue. She lies back down and reaches for my hand. The simple comfort reaches into my brokenness; silent tears weave trails down my cheeks, wetting my neck and tank top.

Minutes…perhaps an hour passes. "Would you think about going to see someone?"

The room seems to expand, grow larger and larger, and I feel like Alice getting smaller and smaller until I can't reach the doorknob to get out. Red pill, blue pill.

"I think so."

When I was eighteen, I got my tattoo. At the time, I believed that I was rebirthing myself in a way, as I lost myself in the BDSM subculture and tried to survive on my own. And in so many ways, I was right.

Somewhere along the way, I lost the idea of rebirth and instead started building walls around my heart, my thinking, and my identity. I drew lines I refused to cross, and instead of liberating me and giving me control, they kept me tied down and afraid.

I guess we all do that at some point, right? When life gets too painful or too hard, we back into a corner and put up our defenses, in hopes of staving off the inevitable hurt.

I'm not sure when the shift happens, but after the first brutal few weeks of therapy where I keep swearing I won't return, things start to turn around. I begin to understand why I ruin relationships (fear of vulnerability), why I'm afraid to be open (afraid to trust the wrong person), and why I have a hard time being out of control (see previous). And as I start to piece together the ruins of my childhood and adolescence, I find an odd emotion surfacing amid the rage and bitterness.

Happiness. With an added dash of acceptance.

But I also discover that a lot of the things that I thought were just "shortcomings" of my personality are actually part of the walls I've built around myself. Sleeping with clients was a way to maintain that numb space, rather than embrace the emotions that overwhelmed me.

I can be both dominant and submissive in a relationship, without betraying the core of who I am and what makes me a good Dom. I don't think I'm a true switch, as I can't see myself fully embracing the submissive role, but knowing that I can let go of the reins and enjoy someone else in control doesn't threaten who I am.

While all of this gives me hope, the reality of my mistakes are a painful blow. Some can be repaired, like the overdue apology to Noah and examining Kinked's future. Other things, though, no matter how much duct tape and glue you bring to the table, can't be reassembled.

Chapter 24
A Spark of Life

"Today is, regrettably, my last session with you, Mistress Hathaway."

I'm in my standard getup, modestly covered in my trench coat, perched on one of the chairs in the living room of the suite.

Charles's handsome face wears his emotions, and I admit to being surprised by his announcement. "I'm sorry to hear that, Charles."

He sits down across from me—carefully, as we had a pretty intense session involving a rubber whip—but he smiles easily. "I hope I'll be back in a few years, but I'm headed overseas for some work in the meantime." He lets a beat pass, then asks, "I've noticed you seem a bit sad, as of late. May I inquire as to why?"

While Charles and I haven't had any heart-to-hearts, he's been very forthcoming about his own struggles in meeting the right woman, and I feel disingenuous not responding in kind. "I've been working on some elements of my mental health recently."

"Good for you." His smile widens. "All of us can use a good tune-up on occasion."

"That's a good way to look at it," I say with a laugh. "I've realized that by not seeking help sooner, I missed out on some once-in-a-lifetime opportunities."

His dark eyes meet mine. "Surely they are not permanently out of the picture?"

I look down at my hands, the nails elegantly polished for the first time in months. "Some things are, unfortunately, permanent."

"I'm sorry to hear that." His smile turns compassionate. "There are other opportunities, though. You are young, beautiful, accomplished."

I aim for a smile, but I fall a bit short. "Yes, there are. I have some new business pursuits that will hopefully be successful."

"I'm intrigued. Will you share them with me?"

I nod, surprised by his interest but glad to be able to gush a bit. "I'm in the process of finalizing a business proposal that I'll be sending out to investors for a sleek, sexy, and discrete dating service that caters to fetishes and alternative sexual preferences. I just hired a graphic designer to do some mock-ups of the website design, and I've enlisted the help of some very business savvy friends to help me. I had an investor—a powerful one—but due to the lawsuit involving that dating service that the serial rapist used, they decided to hold off on moving forward." One corner of my mouth turns up. "Now, it's just a matter of seeing it through and hoping others will have the same vision that I do." Absently, I smooth the edge of my coat over my thigh. "I'm hopeful though. It's something that has been calling to me for a while." I manage half a smile.

"Sounds wonderful. What is your timeline for it?"

Since he seems sincere in his curiosity, I lay it out for him with details. He listens, attentive and thoughtful.

"You've really thought this through." He steeples his fingers, eyeing me as though seeing me for the first time. Then he nods. "I agree—the current trends in online dating for fetishists and BDSM practitioners range from unimpressive to bizarre. You have a forward-thinking plan and a good mind." He nods. "I look forward to hearing more about this." He reaches into his pocket and pulls out a business card. "I leave next week, but I'll let my assistant know to forward your emails to my personal account."

His invitation takes me off-guard, and after a moment, I reach for his card. "I hope you didn't think I told you these things in an effort to 'sell' you on my idea."

"Of course not." He shakes his head. "I can see your excitement and passion. And what you are designing could be of help to me, personally, so I have a vested interest, you could say. I'm very intrigued by this."

"Thank you." I don't know what else to say.

We walk to the door, and he takes my hands. "Mistress Hathaway, I would like to ask you a personal favor."

Curious, I narrow my eyes at him with a smile. "What is it?"

"You mentioned that you lost a rare opportunity, and I have my own suspicions as to what you refer." He glances down at our joined hands before meeting my gaze again, and I am reminded that he must be near sixty, though with his spirit and personality, he has always seemed like a much younger man to me. "Life, as they say, is short. And while you may think that all hope is lost, often, when given a strong wind, it takes flight when we least expect it. Perhaps you might rethink giving up on that 'lost opportunity.'"

I don't say anything, in large part because a lump has formed in the back of my throat. My eyes threaten to well with tears, but I ignore them, focus instead on Charles's tie. After a moment the emotion passes, and I look up at him. "I will consider your request."

He squeezes my fingers with a small nod of his head. "Thank you for my punishment, Mistress Hathaway. I will endeavor to be less naughty for you."

"Take care of yourself, Charles. That's a command. I look forward to hearing from you upon your return."

As I walk away, the wave of emotion returns with a vengeance, and I'm thankful for the privacy of the elevator, where I can let my tears fall without witness.

Chapter 25

Best Laid Plans

"Call him." Ella holds out my phone.

"I can't. This isn't a phone call sort of thing." Mia lies asleep in my arms, her belly full and her chubby cheeks relaxed. Every now and then, I swipe a finger over her cheek, just to see the reflexive smile she offers in response. Which only serves to remind me of someone else who smiles in his sleep.

I sigh. "I have to do this, don't I?"

"Yes, you do," Noah answers, rejoining us in the living room with a wine bottle and two glasses. We're at Ella and Ian's house, supposedly having a night of movies and drinking, except that Ian ended up staying late at the office, and, well, there is a four-month-old in the room. That limits the drinking. And the movie watching.

He pours the wine, handing me a glass and taking one himself. Ella refuses to drink anything until Mia's weaned, and I can't say I blame her. Trying to time drinks while nursing sounds like a feat worthy of Archimedes. So we partake for her, and we're starting on our second bottle.

Noah sits beside me, pulling me back against him, his arm loosely around my shoulder. "Or you could just sleep with me. You know you want to."

"God, you are drunk."

Ella and I say it almost at the same time, and I cheer her with my glass. "Soul sisters."

He rolls his eyes. "Well, just for that, I will deliver a low blow: I might be off the market."

We both stare at him in disbelief.

"Say it ain't so, little bro," she teases.

"It may be. I'm not certain, but I might have met the right woman to cure me of my lascivious ways." He winks.

I'm not sure how seriously to take his claim, so I lean back against him and close my eyes. He's warm, I'm drunk, and I have a sleeping baby in my arms. What gets better than that?

My alcohol-sodden brain is not beyond debating Ella's insistence that I call Fin, though. I want to. God, I really want to. But if I'm going to seek him out one last time, see if there's any hope left, I have to do it in person. I can't apologize without doing at least that. The thought of actually doing it makes me sick to my stomach. Not a good thing when you've had this much alcohol.

I fall asleep listening to the playful, quiet banter of Noah and Ella talking about a problem client, thankful that I have friends with whom I can know what family feels like.

***

Ella offered her car, probably so she could insist on coming with me. "You can't go out there alone. You can drive, since you don't trust my abilities. I'll stay in the car. It will be like I'm not even there."

Mia stayed with Ian, and Noah wished us luck. But the sadness in his eyes didn't bode well.

Eripio Farm seems even farther away than the last time, and my stomach ties in knot after knot as we get closer. Ella lays a hand over mine, which is gripping the gear shift. "It's going to turn out the way it's supposed to, Lux."

I nod, not trusting my voice or emotions. When I pull up outside the barns, I stare out over the acres for a few minutes, gathering my strength.

I glance quickly at Ella for moral support, and she nods. "You can do it."

"What if it's too soon? What if I haven't been in therapy long enough? It's been, what, a month? That's hardly enough time—"

"None of us are perfect, Lux. Just go. Give it a shot."

I exhale. "Yeah. Here we go."

Unlike the last time I was here, the barn is packed with people—children, adults, several dogs. This time, I wore jeans and a sweatshirt, both because I don't want to be noticed, and because I don't want to give Fin anything but my honesty to focus on. I can only hope that's enough. And that he isn't dating someone else already.

That thought definitely gives me pause.

I push one foot in front of the other until I've walked through the barn, past people who aren't familiar to me and don't look like they work here. I'm nearly to the round pen when I see Willie sitting on a hay bale, petting a cat. Grubby, in pants a bit too small for him, he looks up at me. He's lost a tooth, giving him a mischievous expression.

"I remember you," he says by way of greeting.

"You do? I'm glad. Willie, right?"

He nods, then returns his attention to the cat.

"Is Fin around anywhere? I'd hoped to find him."

He looks up at me, one eye squinted against the midday sun. "Nope. He's gone."

Whatever knots my stomach had tightened into quickly turn to wet noodles. "Gone? What do you mean?"

"He went home. Back to Scotland." He over-pronounces it, as though I might not be able to understand him otherwise.

"Really? How long ago?" I don't know why I'm asking. Whatever small dash of hope I'd sprinkled on this venture has dissolved into thin air.

"Dunno. Couple of weeks, maybe?"

I swallow hard. "Thanks for telling me, Willie."

He doesn't respond, and I watch him with the cat for a moment, focused on keeping my breakfast from coming up. Then I walk away.

I step out of the barn, anxious to return to the safety of the car so I can wallow in my grief, but a few horses with riders are entering the barn. It takes a moment, but I recognize the one horse.

"Is this Nellie?" I ask no one in particular.

The girl riding her nods. "Yep, she's awesome."

She's no more than eleven or twelve, and she seems completely at ease on top of the large horse. I reach out a hand towards Nellie's nose, and her lips close around my fingers, seeking a treat. "She is. I saw some of her training."

The girl smiles, nodding. "She's a rescue. We just adopted her, and I love her. She's so awesome." She leans over the buckskin's neck, laying her head on Nellie's mane and stroking the horse's neck.

I don't know much about horse expressions, but Nellie seems pleased enough, and I smile at the girl before heading for the car.

"You are back way too fast," Ella says as I get in.

"He wasn't there." I slip the key in the ignition, listening to the old engine roar to life. "He went home."

She stays quiet until we're out on the road, barreling for the city. "He wouldn't be hard to find, you know. You can still contact him."

I nod, but we both fall quiet. I flip on music, anything to fill my mind with something other than Technicolor pain. It's a long ride back to the city, with only The Smiths' "I Know It's Over" acknowledging the truth.

Chapter 26

Falling into Place

Charles is as good as his word. I receive his email a few days after emailing his assistant with a new business plan, this one laying out my vision for Kinked in my own words, rather than in fancy business-ese.

"I am beyond impressed with your diligence and vision for this project. It would be my honor to take part in this venture. I am prepared to discuss numbers. Let's set up a time. Your servant, Charles." I call, set up a time, and a few days before Christmas, we chat.

"So?" Noah asks when I get off the phone with Charles.

"He wants to contribute half of what I need." I can't help the smile spreading across my face. "His assistant will forward the paperwork this weekend."

Noah hoots and grabs me in a hug, which I return with enthusiasm. "I can't believe it." There's still a lot to do, but half…that's something.

"Dinner is called for." Noah gets on the phone and makes reservations at an exclusive steakhouse. "Helps to have a concierge on speed dial," he says, winking, as it's the concierge from the Parisienne I introduced him to a few weeks ago.

We enjoy a lavish dinner of steak, lobster, oysters, and their signature bacon macaroni and cheese. By the time the server asks if we are interested in dessert, we're both holding our distended bellies.

"Oh my God. I haven't eaten like this in months."

He grins but then looks over my shoulder.

I turn to look, and I'm greeted by the smiling faces of Ella and Ian.

They're both in jeans, and when they reach us, they remain standing.

"We can't stay, as it's date night for us." Ella squeezes Ian's arm, and he leans down to kiss her forehead. "We wanted to stop by and tell you that you have another 50% investor." And then she hands me an envelope. "And Merry Christmas."

"What?" I look up at them, confused.

She leans down and busses my cheek. "I'll let Noah translate for you."

Ian squeezes my shoulder, and then they are shown to their own table, some distance from ours.

Noah smiles broadly. "That," he points to the envelope, "is for you for Christmas." He pauses, then continues. "Investing in your company is a family decision. Ian, Ella, and I are your other investors." He grins. "I figured given that we live together, I can protect my investment."

I recover enough from my shock to make a face at him, but I still can't believe it. "I don't want you guys to feel obligated—"

"It's not an obligation." He holds up a hand. "You are family, but besides that, this is a great idea, Lux, and you are the best person to make it happen. How can we *not* support that?"

I finger the edge of the envelope in my hands, but then tuck it into my small bag. "I'm incredibly grateful." I look up at him, feeling as though the sun has finally broken through the clouds. While their generosity feels overwhelming, if Kinked is successful—and I'm even more determined to make it so—then there are no other people in the world I would want to profit from it more than those I love. And Noah's right: they are family to me, in so many ways.

"Not going to open the envelope, eh?"

"It's not Christmas yet."

His eyes widen. "You don't have to wait for it. God, you were one of those kids who waited to open *everything*?"

I laugh. "Yes, as a matter of fact, I was. I loved Christmas, and everything that came with it. So why rush?"

He snorts, then takes a sip of his wine. "Damn. Ella and I would race to the tree all month, wheedling to get our mom to let us open something early."

"Well, I didn't have a typical childhood," I point out with a shrug. "Besides, where's the excitement if you open everything early?"

Noah shakes his head. "Way too practical a mindset."

On the way home, I lean my head against the subway window, the cool glass easing the commotion inside my head. Having my business plan fully funded means now I'm responsible to not only investors, but to friends. So if I wasn't concerned about making the right decisions before—and I definitely was—I'm even more terrified about getting it wrong now.

My therapist would say something along the lines of, seek out one problem at a time, and deal with that one. Tomorrow will be soon enough to tackle the next one.

Chapter 27

No Place Like Home

One Year Later

Bakertown is a far cry from New York City. If it sounds like sleepy suburbia, that's because it is. I've been driving about two hours, and when I pull off for gas, I consult my GPS to make sure I entered the address correctly. As usual, Stephen lent me his car, and while I don't mind the drive, I'm antsy. Which, given what I'm about to do, is no surprise.

It's another ten minutes, twisting and turning through a flat, surprisingly busy retail highway, before I turn off, heading back into a mixed use area—some executive business centers, a few medical-appropriated buildings, and the occasional restaurant and shopping area.

After parking, I get out and stretch my legs, surveying the terrain. It's a quiet Monday, with few people about. The shopping center has a UPS Store, an Italian Bistro and a few specialty clothing stores, and while I suppose it's technically a strip mall, the elegant design challenges the stereotype. A law office and an interior design firm punctuate the retail theme.

White Peony's front window displays delicate lingerie laid over beds of holiday ornaments and flowers, reminding me that Christmas looms close. It's a small display window, as the store is wedged in the corner, making it easy to miss. I approach strategically, hoping I can peek through the window without being seen.

"Can I help you?" A deep feminine voice asks behind me.

I know exactly who it is, so I turn slowly, unsure what to expect. "Hey, Zi."

She's even more beautiful than I remember, with thick hair like mine, but blonde and wavy as opposed to black and curled. Her father must have been half Viking, I swear, as she got the height and high cheekbones in the family. She retained our mother's light skin, as all three of us did, as well as the full hips. Though unlike me, who's a little too skinny to be classically gorgeous, Zi could be a model had she been born in the time of Marilyn Monroe.

"Lux? Oh my God." Her mesmerizing blue gray eyes take me in. Then she pulls me to her in a hug so hard, I can't breathe.

But I don't complain. It's been a long time.

"Holy shit. I can't believe this." Zi pulled me into her shop's backroom, put a "closed" sign in the window, and made coffee. As she sits across from me now, she can't stop staring at me. "Holy shit."

I smile, but I'm not sure when the bottom of her excitement is going to fall out. "I wasn't sure if you'd be glad to see me or not."

In some ways, her face is so familiar, I want to kick myself for waiting so long to do this. But as she raises an eyebrow now in a way she didn't when she was fifteen, I realize just how long it's been.

"Lux. Jesus. Of course I'm thrilled to see you. It's like Christmas came early this year." She smiles, her slightly crowded teeth now straighter, and her overbite nearly gone. "I lost track of you after college, and I guess…well, I could have looked you up online, I suppose. I didn't think…well, I mean, I didn't know if you'd want that," she finishes, clearly uncomfortable.

"I'm sorry, Zi. Really. I just…after I left, I didn't know how to contact you without being in touch with *him*." I spit out the word, avoiding referring to my foster father by name.

She meets my gaze. "You do not have to explain it to me. Kevin was an asshole." She gets up to pour coffee. She waits until she's seated again to speak. "He's dead now, you know."

"Wow. Really?" Months ago, that would have made me smile bitterly. Now, I'm surprised to find myself a bit numb to the information. "Mama C must be devastated."

Zi snorts. "Hardly. She divorced his ass right before Blue moved out. Well, the *first* time she moved out."

I pour too much half-and-half in my coffee, which causes my heart to ache a bit as I remember someone who loves too much cream in his coffee. But I shake it off. "How is Blue?"

She sips her coffee before answering. "Blue is…well, Blue. Pretty much the same as you remember, probably. Impossible, impetuous, bitter. I'm amazed how such a little person can harbor so much resentment."

My youngest sister was always difficult, even as a child, but she was also adorable and wildly intelligent. At one point, her teachers had suspected her of genius level intelligence, but our mother refused to let her be tested. Once we went into the system…well, nobody worried much about such things. Zi and I were very protective of Blue, but it was hard to get close to her.

"What's she doing now?"

"She keeps threatening to go back to school, but she'd have to actually apply to make that happen. So who knows? She works at Little John's."

I nearly spit out my coffee. "What?" Our grandmother owns Little John's diner and coffee house, but it's not a modern "coffee shop." Think 1950's diner, and you have a pretty good idea of Little John's atmosphere and menu.

Zi gives me a wry grin. "Don't ask me how she does it. I couldn't work for that bitch if you gave me a million bucks. But that's Blue for you. Hates the woman, but it's where she landed, so she puts up with it."

I shake my head. "Damn. I don't even know what to say."

"Then tell me about you."

The wistfulness in her voice surprises me. Somewhere in all my avoidance, I neglected to consider that I might matter to Zi; that not having me around hurt her. I was always too focused on my own damage.

"Well, I'm a business owner. You may have heard of it, actually. 'Kinked' is an online dating service—"

"No! That can't be yours!" she nearly shrieks. "I can't believe it. I just referred two clients to the website. It's brilliant."

I grin, happy that she recognizes my company. "Yes, it's done really well. We've been officially in business for about eight months, and it's been incredible. We're working on our international branding right now, with hopes to be able to expand to that market incrementally over the next two years." It's been unbelievable, really.

She's so rapt as I speak, that I tell her as much as I can about the last twelve years.

"So first you were a professional Dominatrix," she wiggles her eyebrows at me, "and now you run a kinky dating service. Do you still take clients as a Dom?"

"Not anymore. In fact, I just referred my last client a month ago."

"Dear God. Mama C would shit."

"Do you still talk to her?"

She nods. "Not often. I know how you feel, and I totally agree with you—she didn't protect you, or us, really. But…"

"She's weak, Zi. I understand that now. It's not like she meant to hurt us."

"No, she didn't. So I keep in touch, visit her once a year on Thanksgiving. She's all alone now, so I feel like it's a bit of a good deed, if you will."

"It is. At the risk of sounding like an ass, I'm really proud of you."

Her face beams at my comment. "Thanks."

"And apparently, owning our own businesses runs in the family." I smirk.

She laughs, then nods. "Yep. I never thought I could make White Peony work, but it's been two years. I'm even considering expanding and opening another store."

"That's awesome."

We catch up on more details about her life this time, and I learn she's been married and divorced, had three miscarriages, and hated working in public relations, which is what she got a college degree in. White Peony offers custom lingerie fittings, but she sells an assortment of female focused sex items in the back.

It's a relief to actually sit across from her, listen to her stories, and know that she's still my sister, even if I've dropped the ball for all these years.

Before I leave, she takes my hand. "I want you to know something. I understood why you left. It was hard on me, probably harder on Blue, to be honest, as she idolized you."

My eyes widen, and she nods.

"She missed you terribly, but I think even she knew what was going on. Or at least, parts of it. It wasn't your fault, Lux. None of it. And even though I've missed you terribly, I knew you'd come back around when it was time."

"How the fuck did you end up so zen?" I ask, chuckling.

"I don't know that I'm zen, but I had a lot of therapy, and I do a lot of yoga." She flashes me her signature smile. "Seriously. I needed time to process things afterwards too. And then after my divorce…well, let's just say, I needed to get away from everything for a while. I don't want you to feel guilty or bad about things. We weren't your responsibility— we had a mother with a mental illness. Hate her or love her, she couldn't help herself. And you, me, and Blue…we made it. Maybe not as easily as we would have liked, and not without some scars, but we survived."

I clasp her fingers tightly. "Thanks. I've wanted to do this for a long time. I was just…scared, I guess."

I don't want to leave, but she has a bra fitting appointment soon, so we walk to the car. "You know, I've got a Charlie Brown Christmas tree all set up at home. You are welcome to join me for the holidays."

"I'll do you one better. I celebrate with Noah and Ella every year. Why don't you join us? They'll love you, and I'd really like you to meet them. They've been like family to me, and I'm pretty sure we're taking adoptees."

Her eyes brighten. "That sounds lovely."

We exchange phone numbers, and when she hugs me, I can feel the depth of her emotions in her tight embrace.

"Love you, Lux. Always."

I pull her face down to kiss her forehead. "Love you, Zizi Baby." I haven't said her nickname in years, but it rolls off my tongue. "Thanks for not hating me."

My drive home carries mixed emotions. I am beyond thrilled to have seen one of my sisters. I'll reach out to Blue, but according to Zi, she doesn't keep in touch with anyone and is pretty closed off. I'm going to try anyway. One family puzzle piece at a time, though.

Despite my joy over seeing my sister, I can't seem to shake the sadness that clouds my heart. With Christmas approaching, I feel the lack of being "settled," and while I never thought I'd want that for myself, being with someone like Fin awakened that need in me. And I don't know how to answer it yet.

Chapter 28

Decisions

It's three days before Christmas, and Ian and Ella have put on a huge party. Food, gifts, games, as only a professional event planner knows how to do. Because Ian's extended family lives in upstate New York, Ian and Ella decided to do a small, private celebration on Christmas Day and spend the few days prior visiting with family and friends. Ian's mother and father have traveled to Ian and Ella's. They're incredibly gracious people and down to earth, despite their wealth, and I always enjoy being with them. The only thing that would make this holiday more perfect…would be someone that I know I can't have.

It's been a little over a year since I saw Fin last. No contact, not even a text. But then, I'd wanted it that way, for both of us. Watching Ian and Ella, listening to Noah tease us about another possible "serious" girlfriend, holding Mia and watching as she totters around the room now…the moments are bittersweet. I couldn't ask for a more wonderful group of people to be part of, but I'm sad I've made my life this way, that I pushed Fin away when I should have pulled him into me, told him about my issues, been more honest. I wasn't facing things myself at the time, though. Even now, I'm still working through the mess of it all.

We've opened gifts, eaten mounds of food, and we're sitting around the piano singing Christmas songs while Ian's mom plays, when Ella and I break off to set up for games.

"I'm guessing you decided not to take me up on my Christmas gift last year," she says quietly as we stoke the fireplace in the family room before dragging out the tables.

I raise an eyebrow. "What are you talking about?"

"Your gift—the one I gave you that night at the steakhouse. You never used it, so I'm assuming you've made your peace with it."

"I don't...Oh!" I realize she's referring to the envelope she gave me that night. "Shit, I never opened it."

"Lux!" She shakes her head. "How do you forget to open a present?" Her disbelief is tinged with humor. "Where is it?"

I think for a moment. "I think it's still in the side pocket of my purse." Given all that happened this year, getting a new handbag was the least of my concerns, so I'm still using the same one.

I know, I know—don't judge. It's been a busy year.

I find my bag in their coat closet, as well as the slightly crumpled envelope Ella had given me, tucked away in the side pocket. Ripping it open, I discover a tri-folded voucher for a first class, round-trip airfare to the destination of my choosing. I stare at the brightly colored form for several minutes before returning inside.

Ella is prepping the next round of drinks in the kitchen.

"I don't know what to say, Ells." I lay the voucher on the kitchen's island, smoothing the surface over and over again with my hands. "I can't believe I didn't see this."

"I can't believe you didn't, either," she teases, but then she sobers and stands across from me. "I want you to be happy, Lux. If you don't want to be with him, that's fine. But I wanted to make sure there are no excuses."

I step back and meet her gaze. "What if I've waited too long?"

She doesn't say anything.

"I told him I couldn't love him." I shake my head, marveling at my foolishness. "What if I'm still just as screwed up as I was before?"

She lays her hands on my mine, stopping my incessant stroking of the voucher. "None of us are perfect. I wasn't when I married Ian. God, I was a nightmare." We both grin as we recall a drinking bender the night before her wedding, wherein she nearly called it off. "And you are working on your issues. Believe it or not, Fin probably has a few of his own problems beneath all that Scottish hotness and charm. You'll never know if you have a chance to learn and grow and screw up together if you don't go find him."

"What if he's with someone else? Or married?" My stomach rolls on itself at the thought.

Ella, always practical, shrugs. "Then at least you know. And you can let it go, knowing that it wasn't meant to be. Right now, we're just guessing."

I stand there, mulling the enormity of this idea over. "Jesus. I'm going to get on a plane and go do this?" I mean it as a question, but then it's not one. "God, that means I have to fly."

She nods, a smile playing across her lips. "Yep, you are. And you'll white-knuckle it the whole way. And that voucher? It will buy any ticket you want, any day you want it. But it's going to expire tomorrow."

We barely take a breath before we're both scrambling for the study and her laptop.

Chapter 29

Have Yourself a Merry Little Christmas

I flew to Mexico once, the summer after I graduated college. And one of my boyfriends and I headed down to the Caymans a few years ago. Hm…maybe more than a few years…

Nonetheless, I've never been to Europe. I didn't remember how intense international travel was (not to mention my abject fear of being in the air), the questions you get asked at the entry point, the changing planes and airports, and the strangeness of a new culture. In Edinburgh, even though they're speaking English, the thick Scottish burr takes a bit to get used to. When I hear it, my heart squeezes with the memory of another deep, heavily accented voice, and I grip my luggage handle tighter.

The sky is gray with rain, and as I get into my rented car, cold droplets pepper my cheeks.

Kirkliston isn't that far from the airport, but driving on the opposite side of the road takes a bit of focus. After nearly twenty hours of travel—courtesy of a last minute reservation and three connecting flights—I'm running on adrenaline, and I've been awake over twenty-four hours. But my curiosity over my new surroundings wins out. The urban sprawl of Edinburgh gives way to lush farmland. I try to focus on that, rather than the way my heart pounds in my ears the closer I get, and the intense yearning in my gut for balance and an answer to the constant question that tears me up inside.

Is there a chance?

The town of Kirkliston holds tiny homes interspersed with commerce-driven lots, and ancient stone churches, one with a huge stone spire and surrounded by grave sites, greet tourists. I booked a bed and breakfast for two nights. I figured that would be long enough to either find Fin and get an answer…or give up and go home.

Parking on the street, I pull my woolen coat tighter. There's a chill in the air, and I haven't any clue what to do next. You'd think finding someone you love would be easy, especially in our uber-connected culture. In this case, it's a bit challenging. Since Fin doesn't use Facebook or take part in social media, there was little to help me online. His parents own a dry cleaning shop, and I figured I'd start there as there was only one listed in Kirkliston according to my research. It's Christmas Eve, so most places are closed. And now, standing outside the quaint inn I've booked and breathing in the fresh, crisp air, I realize nothing is going to happen without food…and then sleep.

As I walk the narrow streets of this small town, I'm most impressed by how old it is. Living in a city where technology has its own zip code, I don't often see old architecture and crumbling rock. The people are friendly, most nodding and smiling as I pass them. According to my printed map, the cleaners his parents own is just ahead. When I spy the entrance, a sign posted warns that they're closed until the new year.

Seeing that today is Christmas, I'm not surprised. Given that I had only twenty four hours in which to book my ticket, it's not like I had a lot of options. Still…perhaps coming to a strange country with no real leads or contacts was not the best idea.

While on the plane, I'd done some searching for his parents' address, but smart people that they are, all of their information is unlisted. And of course, Fin barely registers on Google. The only saving grace was that he played on a local football team, and the team listed all their players on their website. Whether he still lives here with his folks seems unlikely, but it's all I've got. Kirkliston is a tiny town, so it can't be that hard to find someone, assuming he's still here…

There's enough of a cold breeze to have me scurrying for the only open business on the street: a small restaurant. I order a coffee at the counter and examine the local advertisements.

"Can I get ye anything else, dear?"

I look up at the small woman, her gray hair pulled into a bun on top of her head. "No, I'm fine."

"Sound like ye're a bit of an American, then?"

I smile at her curiosity. "A bit."

She chuckles. "Aye, ye are. Ye're here for pleasure then? A bit of a holiday?"

"No, I'm actually here looking for someone."

"A small town like Kirkliston, I wouldn't think it would be hard to find anyone." She leans her heft against the counter, tucking herself between two stools beside me. I'm the only customer.

"You wouldn't think. Since most places are closed…"

"Who're ye looking for? I've lived here nearly ten years; I can probably help ye."

I take a sip of my coffee. "The MacKenzies who own the cleaners."

She eyes me curiously. "Aye, what do you want them for, then?"

What to say? I decide the truth is the way to go. "I'm actually trying to find Fin MacKenzie. He and I…well, we used to date. A while ago. And I made a bit of a mess of things, so I'm trying to find him and make it right. Or try to, at least." Nothing like sharing one of your biggest blunders with a complete stranger, but the admission lightens the heaviness in my chest.

She pats my hand, a sympathetic look in her eyes. "I've buggered things up a time or two myself, so I ken the feeling. Let's see, MacKenzie's a common enough name around here, and I canna say I know the folks who own the cleaners, but Fin MacKenzie I know well. He's a local footballer, ye ken?"

I nod. "Yes, he is. Does he live around here?"

"Canna say…" She thinks for a moment. "Och, I'm an ol' fool! The local team, they always play a holiday game, unofficial, of course, down on the Douglas's field. Been doing it since my own Samuel was a tyke. Ye should go out there. Ye might find him there, if he's in town for the holiday."

I feel a thrill of hope, but even though I do my best to follow her directions, I lose my way within minutes. So I follow the street I'm on in hopes that it will eventually lead to one of the streets she mentioned. Besides, it's Christmas, and this might be a fool's journey. I should enjoy the day and its brisk air, right? Embrace what comes, as my therapist encourages me to say.

The homes around me are decorated for Christmas, and while there are few people outside, the one or two I see wave and wish me a "Happy Christmas."

Up ahead, there's a wide field, and I hear the unmistakable shouts of men playing a sport. When I round the last house, I discover a horde of them, or so it seems, kicking a black and white ball out in the middle of the empty field. I lose count of how many are on the field, but at least a dozen and a half, playing with focus and abandon, wearing a mishmash of t-shirts, shorts, sweatpants, and even jeans. A few onlookers cheer and coach from the sidelines.

While I've never been much of a sports fan, watching their impressive footwork holds me in place. It's impossible to guess at ages from this distance, but they are agile and quick. I scan the teams, but no one looks familiar. My heart sinks, but then one of them calls out in victory. I would know that voice anywhere. His dark copper hair's long, nearly touching his shoulders, and he's wearing a beanie, so it was easy to miss him. But his height sets him apart, and when he turns, making a play for the ball, I get a clear view of his face. My breath catches in my throat.

He looks, of course, the same, but there's something different about him. I can't place just what. Maybe it's the time apart. I settle against a small shed just off the road, and I can't take my eyes away from the tall baller who's having the time of his life, picking good-naturedly on another player and diving after a ball when he takes over the goalie position. After a half hour or so, I'm frozen to the bone, and I nearly collapse with gratitude when they disperse, collecting shed clothing, and head off en masse towards parked cars. I lose my nerve. I've waited too long to do this. The man I just watched is happy, content, and probably has a girl waiting for him back home. But the fear that I might have made a huge mistake by coming here wars with my need to talk to him, to be in the same space with him.

A last minute decision, I run after them, my Doc Martens not much of a match for their long strides. As they pile in cars to leave, I'm too far away to reach them.

I'm bent over in the middle of the field, trying to catch my breath. "Lux?"

I hear his shout and glance up. Fin steps out of one of the cars. Unsure what to do, I wave, feeling like a fool.

He says something to his friends, then starts towards me. He's in basketball shorts, and he's pulled his leather jacket on over his long-sleeve t-shirt. His face wears a mask of confusion and, thankfully, a slight smile when he finally reaches me. "Lux, what are ye doing here?" His voice holds a bit of wonderment, which gives me hope.

This is the part I didn't plan out very well. "Merry Christmas?" I sound like an idiot.

"Aye, well, yeah, Merry Christmas to ye too." He grins, and shyness rises up between us. "Are ye here for the holiday?"

"Yes. No." I shake my head, trying to clear it. "I'm here for you." I bite my lip. "To find you, I mean."

"Ye found me. Not particularly hard to do in this place." His aquamarine eyes capture mine as they always have, and he steps back. "Ye're going to freeze out here." He shrugs out of his coat, then lifts it over me to tuck around my shoulders.

He smells clean, a little sweaty, and the fragrance I remember tortures my senses. "I don't want to interrupt your time with your friends. I can come back later." Two cars have pulled out, but the others are still there, engines running.

He seems to sense my hesitance, and perhaps even the reason. So he waves to them, shouts something about catching up with them later, and then turns to me. "Let's walk to the diner, then. We can warm up."

We fall into step, and he guides our way. We're silent on the walk, as though we're both a little afraid to break the precious space with words.

Inside the toasty diner, we take a table, and the waitress smiles heartily and winks at me. "I'll get ye some coffee, then."

After she leaves, he eyes me, and I look away. I don't know how to start, even though I rehearsed what I wanted to say on the plane ride.

"Were ye looking to join the football league? Or were ye going to say something?" He chides me lightly, but there's a bit of frustration behind the words.

I glance over at him, then return my gaze to the fork in front of me, twisting it between my fingers. "Sorry. I keep trying to figure out what to say, actually, but everything sounds a bit…ridiculous."

"Why don't ye start with why ye're here?"

"Because I'm an idiot? Because I've missed you every day since I acted like an asshole? Because I should have been honest with you instead of hiding behind my fear?"

He pauses, and when I look up, I'm surprised to find a bit of awe on his face.

"Damn, woman, when ye jump in, ye go all the way."

I raise an eyebrow. "Yeah, well, I was a Dominatrix for a reason."

"Was? Are ye retired, then?" A shadow of his crooked smile appears.

"Something like that." I sigh, then continue. "Kinked—the dating service I was working on—it's doing really well, so it takes up all my time."

"Well then. That's good. Congratulations," he says quietly.

My earlier statement hangs over us, and now it's his turn to fidget, tearing the edge of a napkin.

"Ye said ye dinna love me."

The anguish behind his simple statement hits me like a blow to the stomach. "I know. I'm sorry. I have no excuses for the way I acted. I was fighting you as much as I was fighting myself."

"What changed for ye? If ye couldna love me then, as I loved ye, why is it different now?"

I've struggled with how to respond to this question for the last few weeks, and I've never had a satisfactory answer. Not because I haven't changed my way of thinking, but more because I don't know how to put it into words. And for the first time, I have to do it for more than just myself—I owe it to Fin. "Because I lied to you, Fin. I loved you even then. So much, it scared me. I've never felt that way. I mean, I've been 'in love.' With all the lust and excitement that it entails, sure. But I've never felt for anyone what I felt—feel—for you, and it took my world apart. Who was I if I wasn't independent and a loner? What kind of career could I have and still have a relationship? And so I fought it. I fought you."

"But I never asked ye to change anything."

If I thought I had caused him pain before, the look on his face now…it occurs to me how monstrous I truly was to him. And I'm ashamed. "I know you didn't. This is not your fault. None of it. I had a lot of shit to deal with from when I was a teenager, and honestly, I didn't even know how deep it went. But I'm taking care of it now. I found a therapist, and I'm working through all the crap in my head." I wrap my arms around myself, trying to hold in the tiny amount of heat left as my body chills at the realization that too much damage has been done. I can't repair this. "You didn't deserve any of the crap I put you through. I'm sorry."

He looks at me, his emotions deepening the brackets around his mouth and the wounds in his eyes. "I know ye are. And I appreciate ye coming all this way to tell me that. But I dinna ken what to say. Ye broke me, Lux Trace. And it hurt. I've spent the last year trying to get over ye."

I nod, the tears needling my eyes as I blink quickly, determined not to cry in front of him. "I know. And it's okay. I needed to at least apologize. I realize that it's been a really long time, and you're probably already seeing someone else."

He looks down guiltily.

Damn. I had no idea what it would feel like to have my heart ripped in two, but the pain is magnificent. "Oh, God. I'm so sorry. I shouldn't have—" I wipe at the tears viciously. "No, I should have. I needed to apologize to you. You deserve to be happy, and I hope you are." I reach out, unable to resist touching him one last time, and squeeze his hand, his fingers hot against the ice of mine. Then I shrug out of his coat, leaving it on the back of the chair. With one last look at him, his handsome face a mask I can't quite decipher, I leave the restaurant.

Chapter 30

If At First You Don't Succeed

February

The New Year brings with it a sense of renewal, and while I can't say I'm feeling particularly hopeful about my love life, I'm determined to make a fresh start.

Kinked has exploded, and I have a huge staff—well, to me, it's huge. Divine, Inc. has even contacted me about investing, but I've been putting them off. Noah's back to his womanizing ways, and though I've asked a few questions, he clams up, so I let him go. Far be it from me to be telling someone how they should live.

I live part-time in the city, actually. Zi and I have been testing out being roommates, and so far, it's going pretty well. It's nice to see her more. But I've been a city girl for too long to give it up entirely. Noah says he's sharing custody of me.

I've tried dating. Twice. With less than stunning results. Running a dating service certainly makes it convenient, but my luck at love's as fickle as the next person's, I guess. As I told my therapist, I'm trying to trust that when the time is right, I'll meet the right person. In the meantime, I have vibrators.

Oh, and Noah got a puppy. I'm not sure if it's something to do with women being attracted to men with dogs—though, given that Noah's a hottie, he needn't worry—but it's a little rescue pup named Tag, so when I'm home, we take turns letting him out.

It's Valentine's Day, but I'm trying not to think about it. I've got plenty of spreadsheets that need attention, web design drafts that need to be reviewed, and Tag is determined to ruin my concentration with his dark little eyes and determination to step all over my keyboard.

Noah peeks his head into the living room. "Hey, can you hang around the place for a little bit? Tag hasn't pooped yet, and I don't trust him, do I, little man?" Noah addresses the dog with a singsong voice.

Tag glances up at him from his resting place on my lap, where he's batting at my hands as I type. I ruffle his ears, then stroke his silky head. "I got Tag-watch for this afternoon. What time will you be back?"

"An hour? Maybe two?"

"Lunchtime fuck, or an actual date?"

Noah's mouth presses into a flat line of mock indignation. "Just for that, I will give you no details, you evil wench." He flounces out the door dramatically, making me laugh.

Tag watches me curiously but is easily satisfied with a tummy rub, and I return to reading emails. Within minutes, though, there's a knock at the door. Tag hasn't quite got the hang of barking yet, so instead, he whimpers and looks up at me.

"I know, killer. I'll take care of the big bad visitor." I deposit him in the kitchen, which is gated off to prevent against messes on the living room carpet, then head to the door.

I nearly swallow my tongue when I see who it is.

He's cut his hair. It's not short, but gone are the long curls that I saw in December. He's freshly shaven, and he wears a blue sweater and trendy jeans, with leather sneakers, a backpack hanging from one shoulder. It's such a different look for him, but I couldn't care less as I meet his gaze.

"Hello," he says softly.

"Hi." I memorize his face while my heart pounds in my ears.

"Do ye happen to know where a tourist can get a coffee nearby? I seem to have lost my way."

I'm not sure how to answer that. "Um..."

He chuckles, taking a step back self-consciously. "Aye, now that it's my turn to start the conversation, I seem to have the same problem ye did." But when his eyes meet mine, the questions there need no words.

I'm fresh-faced, still in last night's pajama pants, and I'm not even sure that I brushed my teeth this morning. That doesn't stop me from pulling his mouth to mine. When his arm encircles me, I lean into him, exploring him hungrily. He holds me against him, stepping inside so he can close the door behind us.

His hands seek out flesh, slipping beneath my hoodie. I unzip it for easy removal, and then tug at his t-shirt. We're naked and breathless in less than a minute, and when he lifts me, I wrap my legs around him. Pressing me against the foyer wall, he slides into me slowly.

"Holy fuck," I whisper against his neck, feeling impossibly full. I gasp when he starts to move, but then he kisses me, holding my ass so he can reach into me even deeper. I cling to him, unable to take a full breath as sensation takes over.

Sandwiched between him and the wall, I can't move as he pulls out, then drives into me again, this time with force. He cups my jaw, looking into my eyes as he thrusts again. And again. Until finally his mouth savages mine as we get lost in the rhythm.

When the intensity is too much, he carries me to the couch. I straddle him and sink my fingers into his hair, pulling his head back so I have unrestricted access to his mouth. With punishing slowness, I rock my hips, reveling in the feel of him, the slick connection that's driving our desire. When I can no longer take anymore, I ride him hard, overtaken by white-hot pleasure as his hands curl over my shoulders, holding me against him as he finally shudders his own release.

When I slip off of him, he pulls me down to the couch, stretching out beside me.

"That was a lot easier than starting the conversation." He lifts up on one elbow so he can trace my cheek with a finger. "But I still have a few things to say to ye."

"I'm listening." I reach for the throw on the back of the couch and spread it over us.

He ponders for a moment. "Aye, well, ye see, when ye came to Scotland—and I ken it was no small feat for ye. I remembered that ye hated to fly. So I knew a powerful thing drove ye to see me. But, damn, Lux, ye messed me up, love. I withdrew my application to college, left my internship, and went home, just to figure out how to get over ye. My poor mother had to put up with me living back under her roof—and believe me when I say, she had no love for her prodigal son taking up in her newly furnished sewing room." He chuckles, but then sobers. "I'd just started seeing someone, and there ye stood, reminding me all too well of how much I still cared for ye." He tangles his fingers with mine, then presses my knuckles to his lips. "It killed me to watch ye go, but ye had truly shocked me. I had no idea ye still even thought of me."

"God, Fin, I am so sorry. I don't even have a good excuse—"

"Hush now." He covers my mouth with our joined hands. "Let me finish. As I was saying, I'd just started seeing someone. And she is a verra nice woman. So I couldna even entertain what ye'd said until I figured out what I was doing with her, ye see."

My heart squeezes at the thought of him with someone else. "I take it that's addressed, then?"

A corner of his mouth turns up as he gazes down at me. "She is a verra nice woman, but she's not ye, Lux. And I knew I was leaving, ye ken? So how fair would that have been?"

"Leaving for?"

He exhales, then kisses me hard on the mouth. "If ye'd let me finish what I was saying, this would be a lot easier."

I chuckle, then nod. "Proceed."

He looks at the ceiling. "Dammit, woman, I can't remember where I was."

"You were saying something about another woman."

"Ye would remember that part, eh? Aye, I had to straighten out that part of things, which was easy enough. We'd been out a few times while I was home, but since I was returning to the States, there wasn't much more discussion to be had. And before ye ask, I was accepted at Cornell's veterinary program. I started in January."

"That's awesome! Congratulations!" I lean forward to kiss him, and he indulges me, but then pushes me back.

"But as I was saying…fuck it, I can't even remember what I was going to say."

He thinks for a moment, and I revel in the warmth of him beside me. I have no idea what happens next, but this feeling, the rightness of him beside me is all I need for now. I draw his face down to mine, kiss his lips with as much gentleness as possible. "I love you, Fin. I am sorry that I—"

"Stop. I dinna want to hear that ye're sorry. Ye already said it. This isn't all yer fault. Ye dinna ask to be hurt or mistreated. And I know ye dinna mean to take it out on me. I'm only sorry that it happened to ye." He lifts my hand and kisses my palm before laying it over his heart.

"I've loved ye since the first night ye yelled at me in the hotel."

"Oh God," I say, my cheeks heating up. "I was such a shrew."

"Aye, but I was determined to make ye *my* shrew," he teases.

I stick my tongue out at him, but then he kisses me until I can't take a full breath.

"Unfair diversion."

He smiles at me. "So, I have a plan in mind, if ye're game?"

I nod, feeling a warm flutter in my heart.

"We start fresh. Give this another good go. But," he punctuates the word with a hard gaze, "we have to promise two things to each other."

"Agreed."

"I dinna even tell ye what they are yet."

I grin, but then count them off on my fingers. "One: I will always respond to your texts or calls, even if only to say I can't talk right now. And two, I will tell you when something upsets me, even if it seems minor."

He blows out a breath. "Damn you, woman. Did ye turn psychic on me while I was gone?" He kisses me hard, then hops off the couch. "I nearly forgot. I have a present for ye." He returns moments later with his backpack. "I dinna know when I bought this over a year ago that it would end up having as much meaning as it does." He withdraws a long white box, similar to what flowers might come in, but not quite as wide or long, with a dark blue ribbon tied around the middle.

He hands the box to me. "Do ye remember our first date?"

I finger the ribbon. "You mean when we went to the kid's restaurant?"

He chuckles. "Aye, well, that's not the part I meant." He gestures to the box. "Open it."

I eye him with mock suspicion as I untie the ribbon. Amid tissue paper lies a beautiful leather cuff with a hand-painted peacock feather, nestled beside the real thing.

"Ye said that night that the peacock represented rebirth, another chance to get things right," he says softly.

The cuff's leather feels like butter, and I handle it gently, admiring its beauty.

His fingers graze my shoulder, outlining the curves of my tattoo. "Perhaps that's what we do now."

I fasten the cuff around my wrist, then lean forward, pressing my mouth to his in a slow, sensual kiss. "You are my rebirth." I smile through the tears that threaten. "I've never met anyone who loves the way you do, without reserve or fear. And I want to be able to give you that in return." I press a finger to his lips when he starts to say something. "I lost myself somewhere along the way, and you showed me the way back. It took me a little while to find it," I grin wryly, "but I did. It's my goal that you will never have to doubt my love for you again." When our mouths meet, a promise lingers, and I sink into it happily.

A cry from the kitchen informs me that I have ten seconds before I'm cleaning up a mess. "Crap. I'm coming, Tag!" I call out to the puppy. "We have a puppy now. Technically, Noah does."

"Is that so?" Fin watches me curiously as I struggle back into my pajama pants and hoodie as I rush towards the kitchen. I manage to let Tag out in time, and Fin joins me as I walk the puppy down the block.

"Did Noah know you were coming?"

He slides an arm around my waist. "Aye. He warned me I might have waited too long. And he said something about not hurting ye, or he'd shove his foot up my arse, I believe was the way he worded it."

I grin. "That sounds like Noah."

"He loves ye, as though ye were his sister."

Reaching down, I extract a leaf from Tag's mouth. "Honestly, I couldn't ask for a better family. Noah and Ella, Zi and Blue—whom you'll have to meet," I lean against him, looking up into his eyes. "And you. I don't think it gets much better."

He brushes his lips against my forehead. "Aye, and ye'll have a whole new family to meet in Scotland. Not to mention, quite a few of 'em remember you from your run across the field on Christmas."

"Oh God."

He chuckles against my hair. "Ye definitely intrigued them."

"You have school for at least four years, right? Plenty of time to forget about that."

He chuckles. "Och, did ye learn nothing in history class, love? Scots have terrible long memories."

I am so screwed.

The End

The second book in the Without a Trace series, coming in Summer 2015!

What if I've been wrong about everything... And he's the only thing that's right?

I've never believed in love at first sight, which is probably why I write mysteries, and not romances, for a living. Besides, I'm too focused on expanding Elementary, a mystery dinner party business I own with my brother Noah. I don't have time for romance.

When the handsome and successful Ian Crane books our services, I can barely keep my wits about me. He's setting fire to all my rules, and I can't resist his flames.

I don't recognize the woman I'm becoming, but I don't want to go back to who I was. There's a part of me that can't help wondering, what if he's too good to be true? Because if he is, my heart will be nothing more than ashes.

Ella and Ian's story coming in Summer 2015! Read on for a sneak peek...

Crossing the Line

CHAPTER ONE
What if?

I've always believed that we have a soul mate, and that when we meet them, inside, we'll know. Crazy, isn't it? Surely we'd have been born with some kind of homing beacon, something to lead us to them, if that were the case?

Yet I can't shake it. Every time I meet an old couple who've made it through the storms, or two people who have that unique bond where they finish each other's sentences and seem to live only in their shared world...I'm convinced I'm right.

The problem: what happens when you've already met them, and now they're gone?

"You're sure you don't want to join us afterwards? Meet-and-greets only take a half hour, max." Noah glances at me from across our desks in our dining-room-turned-home-office. We run a dinner-theater company—Elementary—out of our apartment, and while we've got a ways to go before we're a success, we're finally in the black—enough that Noah and I can work for ourselves full-time, rather than have side jobs to pay the bills.

"I've got the meet-and-greet with Ian Crane tonight, a marketing event in the morning, two meet-and-greets tomorrow, and last-minute planning for the party on Saturday." I look up into my brother's deep blue eyes, ringed with silver, just like mine. "I'm absolutely positive

I don't want to meet you and Lux at some dance club or murky bar, wherein y'all will pick up bed partners and I'll come home alone. Weird how it just doesn't appeal to me, eh?"

He sighs dramatically. "Sister dear, you put a little bit more effort into that sexy secretary look you've got going on there, and you'll also be coming home with a little something warm for your very cold bed." He points a finger at my nose. "And you forget, Lux is off the market. She and Evan are doing the holy handholding."

My brother's skepticism around romantic commitments is legendary, though I know he likes Evan. The guy's nice enough, a sweetheart really, and a good submissive to her dominant preferences. But he's not who I thought she'd end up with somehow.

"My lovelies, I've arrived. Where's my party?" Lux waltzes in our front door, decked out for the night in patent leather pants and a crimson corset, her jet-black hair pulled up into a high ponytail. Did I mention she's a professional Dominatrix?

"Your party is about to start, Lulu," Noah greets, standing to buss her cheek and using his pet name for her.

"Any chance my favorite writer is joining us?" Lux pulls me out of my chair and hugs me, enveloping me in her soft, sensual fragrance.

I squeeze her back. "I wish I could. But alas, I have to work. Someone's gotta keep this business going." I wink at Noah, and he grabs his chest.

"I'm injured, dear sister. How could you say such a thing?" He slaps his laptop shut and reaches for his leather jacket. "I fear I'll need several libations to salve my wounded soul."

I roll my eyes at his drama. "Please. Some pretty young thing will do the job just as well."

"Very good point," he agrees, slinging an arm around my shoulders. "Sure we can't change your mind?"

"Evan's going to meet us there," Lux interjects. "And we'll no doubt need someone to keep your brother's seat warm between trysts."

Noah grins, perfectly happy with his reputation as a Don Juan.

"Nope. Already told Mr. Crane I'd be there at eight. So you two go. Tell Evan I said hi. And Lux, try to keep my brother out of too much trouble. I'd rather we not have a repeat of last weekend." I give my brother a pointed look.

Noah's grin fades a bit, and Lux winks at me. "I'll do my best, but he's your gene pool, darling. I have a feeling 'trouble' is in your blood."

I snort as they close the door. If that's the case, it certainly skipped over my DNA. I'm the furthest from trouble you can find.

I miss them as soon as the door closes behind them. They're probably heading out to Noah's favorite haunt, East-West. I'm pretty sure the bartender knows them on sight: Lux isn't exactly forgettable with her viper sexuality. And while Noah's my brother, I haven't missed the fact that he's hot with his dark curls and easy smile.

I've gone out with him and Lux often enough to know how these things go, and I love them both dearly. But I'm over the whole midweek night out. Because the three of us work non-traditional work schedules, Noah and Lux are convinced we must take full advantage of it on a regular basis.

As I pack my cross body bag and double-check my makeup, my shadowed gaze reminds me again why I stopped "partying." A broken heart doesn't make for boisterous company.

Ian Crane lives on the Upper East Side of Manhattan, not far from, thankfully, the subway stop. One track was closed down, so I had to change trains three times just to get here. I left early enough that I'm just barely on time. I take the steps up to the front entrance, and the door opens as I'm cresting the last stair.

It's a good thing I'd already established my footing on the landing, as otherwise I might have tripped. One of the most stunning men I've ever seen stands before me: deep gold, too-long hair brushes his wide jaw in a way that you typically see in magazines, a perfectly cut suit sets off his broad shoulders and narrow waist, and dear God, all I can think is that Adonis must have been reincarnated into this man.

"Mr.—" My mind goes blank, and I have to stare down at the folder in my hands to read his name. "Crane?"

"Ian, please. You must be Ella Storm." He holds the door wide, beckoning me inside. "Come in."

Even his voice is sexy, with a deep, rich tone that makes me think he could read the dictionary, and I would want to listen.

His house is...well, let's just say, my Brooklyn apartment could fit in here five times and still have room left over. The rooms are spacious, well designed, and modern.

"You needed to see where we're going to have dinner, right?" He quirks an eyebrow at me.

The problem with incredibly good-looking guys is that I can barely function around them. I find my tongue and push the words out. "Yes—sorry." I pause, searching for something to say. "You have a beautiful home."

"Thanks." He meets my gaze with a warm smile, and I drop my eyes to my folder. I just have to get through this without embarrassing myself, like, say, slobbering over our new client.

He guides me to the dining area in the open floor plan, showing me how he hopes everyone can be seated, and yet still take part in the show.

We're used to working in typical New York City apartments: cramped, over-loaded with furniture, with little room to set up props. I say as much to him. "This will feel like we're on a Broadway stage."

With a grin, he offers me a seat so we can go over the itinerary. While his party isn't for another two weeks, I like to make sure all the details are in place long before the actual date. We're halfway through the food selections when he reaches for my hand. "This is stunning," he comments as he lightly rests his fingers on my knuckle.

The touch surprises me, and I swear, I can feel the electricity crackle between us. My cheeks flare with heat as I extend my hand so he can admire my ring. The wide, white gold band holds a chocolate diamond, the stark design softened with curved edges and a slightly buffed finish. "Thanks. It was my mom's wedding ring."

His eyes turn knowing. "Was?" When I nod, something in my expression must give me away. "I'm sorry. I lost my dad not too long ago."

"Then I'm sorry as well."

With a strange expression, he stands. "Can I show you something?"

"Of course."

"It's upstairs, if that's okay."

"The actors will need to get dressed somewhere," I point out as I follow him towards the stairs in the center of the room, the only divider between the dining and living room area.

He leads me to a small room just off the steps. The interior has been softened with muted plum paint and comfortable furnishings. A large desk butts up to an expansive window overlooking the back courtyard, and to the right hangs a framed comic book.

"This was my dad's."

I lean closer. "*The Amazing Spiderman*. Oh, it's the first issue." The edges are ruffled a bit from wear, and the ink has long since faded to a patina of washed out shades.

"It's my prize possession. My dad gave it to me when I was eight, and I've loved Spiderman ever since." His smile turns shy at his admission. "I have a lot of my dad's things, of course. But this...well, I'm guessing it's a bit like your ring."

I smile, appreciating his sensitivity. "Both my parents died when I was twelve. My brother was eleven. It was a car accident, drunk driver... you know the drill."

His eyes widen in sympathy. "God, I'm sorry. That had to be impossible. My dad passed a couple of years ago. One day he was fine, and the next day, he was gone. Heart attack."

It's a odd thing, the connection that shared sorrow offers. One moment you're strangers, and the next, you have some intangible link that brushes aside the unknown and allows deeper communication.

"What about your mom?"

"She's actually doing pretty good, now. I didn't know if she'd bounce back. No relationship is perfect, but they were one of those couples that just 'got' each other, you know?"

I nod. "I do."

"She finally met someone—they just got married a few months ago."

"That's great that she was able to find someone again."

"I'm happy for her. And he's a great guy. Nothing like my dad, though, which...I don't know why I'm telling you this." He offers a wry grin. "I actually just got home from work. Must be the hunger talking."

I check my watch. "I'm sorry to keep you. It's getting late. Let me just show you one more thing…"

He touches my arm lightly as I step towards the door, and when I turn around, there's something in his expression that makes my insides curl with desire.

"Are you hungry?"

"Um…" I stall, not sure what to say. While I've had a client or two try to ask me out, I've never wanted to say yes...until now. Aren't there business rules about that somewhere? Still, I'm tempted. But I take the smart way out. "I haven't eaten yet, but I'm going to grab something on my way h—"

"There's a sushi place just around the corner. We could finish going over whatever it is we need to there, couldn't we?"

I'm not sure how we got from dead parents to eating raw fish, and I'm fumbling for an answer. "I guess we could. I—"

His smile widens, interrupting my train of thought. The man's got teeth worthy of a toothpaste commercial.

Within minutes I find myself ensconced in a dimly lit restaurant, a cup of sake in hand, and a delicious man across from me. I really wish I would have worn my dress pants and high heels, as I'm pretty sure I caught Ian checking out my ass as I shed my coat when we reached our table. He was careful to meet my gaze when I sat down, though, so I'm not sure. I could be imagining it.

Don't get me wrong: I know I'm not bad to look at. I won't win any beauty pageants, mind you, but I have a symmetrical face, dark brown, curly hair, and typical, Midwest features. I'm what most people refer to as "cute" or "pretty." Never gorgeous or stunning, like they say about Lux. I carry a bit too much weight in my thighs, and despite my efforts at Victoria's Secret, no pushup bra is going to make my B-cups into Ds. Still, I find myself warming inside at his possible notice.

Probably has something to do with the long swig of sake I just imbibed though, too.

"Can I ask you a personal question?" he asks after we've discussed the last of the plans for his party on Saturday.

His query surprises me, but I nod, curious what he might ask.

"How did you get the idea to start something like this?" He gestures to the folder between us, enclosing his event details. "This is brilliant, but—forgive me if this is presumptuous—you seem very young to have committed to something this..." He struggles for words.

"Adult?" I grin when he looks uncomfortable. "It's okay. You aren't the first person to ask me that. I just look young." I toy with the napkin on my lap. "I'm actually twenty-seven, and this is kind of...a brain child between me and my brother. His idea, really, but we both fell in love with it."

He appears interested, so I keep going. "We were in college—our last year."

"You're twins?"

I shake my head. "We're a year apart, but after our parents died... well, we've always been really close. So I waited to start college. We both wanted to go to NYU, and the expense of staying on campus...well, it just made sense for us to do it together." The explanation has become so pat, even I believe it.

"And you loved the city enough to stay, eh?" His sherry-colored eyes never stray from my face, and the attention heats my cheeks.

"Noah loves it here. He felt like he came home when we arrived. And I like it."

He chuckles. "But you don't love it."

"I don't. But I'm thankful I'm here. Where else could I start a business like this and have it be this successful in such a short time? Don't get me wrong—we've been working on Elementary for years now. We had the idea when we were in our last year of college, but it was a huge undertaking. We've only been officially 'in business' for the last two years, and my brother and I were able to quit our other jobs not quite a year ago so we could focus on this one hundred percent." I'm not sure if I should be telling a client this, but it tumbles out before I can stop it, and the admiration in his gaze makes my insides tingle a bit. Outside of Lux and the people who work for and with us, I don't often get to gush about my pride and joy.

"You work out of your home?"

"Most of the time I work out of a coffee shop." I grin. "But yeah, between there and our dining room that we converted into our office, it's pajamas all day for the win."

"Incredible. Truly. When I was an undergrad, I was more focused on getting a new flat screen television for my first apartment. I hadn't even thought about going out on my own."

"But you went to law school—that's no small thing."

We're interrupted by the server delivering our order, and we take a moment to get acquainted with the chopsticks and enjoy first bites before he takes up his tale again.

"Law school was expected. My dad was a doctor, my mom an accountant with her own firm. Everyone just assumed I'd keep going to school. And don't get me wrong, I love what I do. I'm well-suited to being an attorney, and I've been privileged to have incredible opportunities with my firm, but I never gave it much thought. Not like you and—Noah, right?" He confirms before continuing. "What you two did, and that it's been successful...that's amazing." After a bite of sashimi, he asks, "So where do you get your mysteries? Is that something that you buy, or do you contract to have them written?"

I can't help the small smile that curves my mouth. "Um, I write them," I say softly.

He drops his chopsticks on his plate. "Get out. Really? I've heard awesome things about your stuff. A friend of mine—the one that referred me to you—he said it was like having a professional stage show put on in your living room."

"Noah acts in them as well."

"You two are like the Wonder Twins. Write, act, manage a successful business." He ticks them off on his fingers. "Is there anything you don't do?"

I think about it a moment. "We both stink at cleaning our apartment."

He laughs, a deep, resonant sound that I want to lean into. "I daresay that won't be an issue when you make it big. You can hire someone to do that."

"I have it on my list as the first thing to do when we can afford it."

When we're finished, we both are slow to leave, so we set a relaxing pace back to his apartment.

"Where would you live if you could live anywhere?"

"Austin, Texas," I say without hesitation.

He glances down at me. "I'm betting that's home for you both? That accent is definitely not from the East Coast."

"Born and raised."

"Why didn't you go home after college? Why stay here?"

I can't tell him my real reason, so I come up with the next best answer, which is also largely true. "Noah wanted to stay," I say simply. "There was no way he could afford it on his own, and we had the idea for Elementary, so it made sense at the time."

He nods, but the way his gaze meets mine as we near his building, he seems to know that's not the whole answer. "Well, I'm glad you did. It looks like my birthday party is going to be amazing."

"It will be. No one's seen this mystery yet, so you're the very first one. And it's the best one I've written yet." All the actors told me when they read it that I'd outdone myself, and secretly, I agreed.

At his door, he glances from the entrance to me. "Would you like to come in for coffee?"

I can't get to my watch between my sweater, coat, and gloves, but I know it's getting late. "I should probably be getting back."

He nods, looking away. Then he meets my eyes with a charming grin. "I just got a new coffee maker from my aunt in Italy. I'm told it's one of the best in the world. You might regret missing out on experiencing a cup."

A shy laugh escapes me, and I hear myself say, "I wouldn't want that."

"Neither would I," he agrees and holds the door.

Want more *Crossing the Line*?

Click here to preorder it now!

Acknowledgements

Things happen for a reason, and while I had no plan for this book as I looked out at my writing career, now that it's finished, I'm quite in love with it. It's the product of an unexpected and thankfully short-lived collaboration, but the result of which reminds me why I write: you never know what will come of it.

As every author owes their success to those that came before them, I can only stand in the shadows of the many authors who've shaped my writing over the years. There's too many to name, too many titles that are lost from memory…but those words affected who I am as an artist, and I'm forever grateful.

This story came about because of my determination to write it, but it's in your hands because of the unflappable Patricia D. Eddy, author and editor, who helped me polish this book baby until she shone. Audrey Maddox, my fearless and incredibly supportive friend, proofread this book so I could rest assured that we'd caught as many typos as possible—no book is ever perfect. But we certainly tried.

Jane, my first reader: you rock, lady. Thank you for threatening to smack people around for me. You are truly a kickass woman.

Shari Ryan has been my constant companion in learning the finer elements of Photoshop, and while I designed this cover, she cheered me on.

To my early readers, thanks so much for reminding me that I have a gift. You are the best Sooper Sekrit readers ever!

And to my friends whose words long to see the light: hang in there. Your time will come.

My beauteous partner-in-crime and life, William D. Prystauk, thanks for your faith in me. You're the best.

Ally Bishop, Author

When you do something effortlessly and people commend you continuously, you have found your gift.

That's what I tell people all the time. And it's true.

I get story. I always have. I started writing when I was 8 on a Smith Corona (the electronic kind — I'm not THAT old). I wrote stories in every spiral notebook I had. Eventually, I graduated to a Mac (yes, I'm one of THOSE people). I imagined new worlds, emotional conflicts, and HEAs while I waited at stoplights or wandered the grocery store. But here's the thing: I didn't just dream it up and write it down — I critiqued what I read. I knew when ideas were good, and when they stunk. I ran writing groups, judged creative contests, and eventually got two graduate degrees in writing. That's right: I love it that much.

So here I am, years later, writing kickass heroines and devastating good guys, along with some mystery and vampires thrown in (I promise: THEY'RE COMING). And what's really cool? I do what I love. Wanna write a success story for your life: I promise you, that's it. Do what you love. And hopefully, you can make a living at it too. That's the golden ticket, Charlie.

And chocolate doesn't hurt, either…

Find me at www.allybishop.com, on Twitter (@allyabishop), and Facebook (Ally Bishop, Writer), and feel free to email me via my website (look for the "Contact" tab!)

Thank you so much for reading *Inside the Lines*! If you have a moment, please leave a review on your favorite book websites.

Made in the USA
Middletown, DE
07 March 2015